Bits & Pieces

The Maple Grove
Writers' Studio
Anthology

Bits
&
Pieces

Edited by Marj Helmer

Bits & Pieces

Marj Helmer, Editor

Maple Grove Writers' Studio Anthology

Bits & Pieces: Maple Grove Writer' Studio Anthology

Copyright © 2019 by Marj Helmer

Marj Helmer
7463 Shenandoah Ln N
Maple Grove, MN 55311
Book Layout ©2017 BookDesignTemplates.com
Bits & Pieces/ Marj Helmer—1st ed.
Cover art by Sybil Swanson
Word images from Canva.com and
Images from Pixabay.com
"Magpie Treasures" painting by Caroline Munro
Back cover photos by John S. Maciejny of Natural Images
Clipart from Teachers Clipart
Clipart from Surfer Kids Clipart
Complied by Carolyn Wilhelm
ISBN 9781709390524
Copyright applied for November 2019
Library of Congress Control Number:2019919247

Contents

ACKNOWLEDGEMENTS

Thank you to all the members of the Maple Grove Writers' Studio who bravely submitted their works to this anthology, "Bits and Pieces." A very special thank you to Carolyn Wilhelm for guiding us through publication on Amazon.

Life is continuous learning and we enjoy working together each in our own style and with our individual talents. There is a lot of sharing and support at our studio. Critiquing is positive and kind. Together we grow as writers.

Marj Helmer, Editor

INTRODUCTION

*About the Maple Grove, Minnesota Writers' Studio
Anthology for 2019*

The Writers' Studio of Maple Grove has assembled this anthology for 2019. We have collected "Bits and Pieces" of our work for you to enjoy. Fiction, memoir, poetry, flash fiction, and nonfiction. We include prompts we all suffered and comments about our experiences together. We share inspiration and joy as a writing group. We find support and critiques from each other.

We also have rules, most of them "Sybil's Rules," to keep us positive. No self-criticism, no negativity, start critiquing with good comments, always applaud the writing and the courage to read. Oh, and have fun!

We meet at the Maple Grove Arts Center in a northwestern suburb of Minneapolis, Minnesota, from 11 to 2 every Wednesday.

Read and enjoy our work! AND share the joy with your friends and family.

Our Writers' Studio started in 2018, when two volunteers at the Maple Grove Arts Center spent overlapping shifts together, just chatting. Caroline Munro and Marj Helmer dreamed of studios where artists and writers could join together to enjoy their interests and talents. Caroline designed a webpage and logo, and Marj placed an ad with the Loft, a regional writing center in downtown Minneapolis. Mary Lundeen was the first recruit. She was a psychologist dreading retirement and hoping to develop non-scientific writing skills. Then, a couple of non-writers joined us to see what was going on. We have gained and lost members since, but we still meet every Wednesday to share our writing interest.

We average 8 to 10 members. We have lost members to jobs and gained members from other groups. We are awed by the talents of our members. Besides writing skills, they bring editing, publishing, and experience. When we considered what we had together, we decided to assemble this anthology.

Marj Helmer, Editor

I Used to Call Myself
English

English

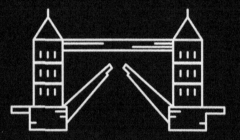

Caroline Munro

I Used to Call Myself English

By Caroline Munro

I'm driving along in my all American, four wheeled drive, big truck. The radio is on, tuned to my kids' favorite station. All is well with my world. I'm enjoying the journey, watching the strip malls zip past my window, obeying the road rules. I'm living the American dream, aren't I? Suddenly a startling thought comes into my mind. "I don't belong here…. I'm a foreigner here. These are not my people and this is not my landscape." My sense of comfort in this world has been rudely ripped away in one second of uncensored thought.

This happens to me less and less now. I am, after all, nine years into this pioneering experience. One change of country, England to the United States, three changes of state, Georgia, Illinois and Minnesota. And six homes later. This is my reality. I can convince myself pretty well, most of the time, that this is normal. But the most unlikely sources can trigger a heart stopping feeling of rising panic that tells my inner self, "Wake up! What are you doing here? This isn't how it's supposed to be!"

When I first arrived in the United States every nerve in my body vibrated with my freshness and vulnerability. I felt like my protective skin had been peeled away as if I had a bad case of sunburn and that my newly revealed pinkness was slowly adjusting to this new way of living. When you have lived in the same place for your whole life, you build up a protective layer of skin that slowly dulls your senses. There is little to excite you or cause you to question the world around you. You have seen and experienced it all before. Everything is familiar and the layers of history, geography and social strata are easily understood and accepted. But, when you are plucked out of this comfort zone and placed in another country, even one that shares a common bond of language, reality shifts and distorts. You have to look and listen harder to your new place. You are dazzled by everything, attaining a crescendo of stimulation. The commonplace takes on a bizarre and amazing twist. The grocery store, a trip to the doctors, a neighborhood coffee morning, are all an education, a chance to fit the story together, to try and find a common denominator that unravels the secrets of life in a different country.

My time in the United States has been rather like a vacation without an end. We have moved house or location every few years and have been able to avoid complacency or boredom with our homes. But there is a part of me that will always remain English, my heart. It still misses a beat when I hear an English voice in a grocery store. I'll study a child's clothes whilst eating in McDonalds. Guessing quite rightly that they are English, probably 'Clark's' shoes and a 'Marks and Spencer's' T-shirt. Desperately I'll search through my handbag for a pen and paper to offer the child's parent my address and a friendly 'port of call' if ever they need it.

I'll flick impatiently through the TV channels looking for 'Masterpiece Theatre,' 'The Antiques Road Show' or I will listen to anything delivered in an English accent on CNN no matter how irrelevant or boring.

My heart beats with pride when I see an English reporter standing in the rubble of Bosnia, Kabul, or war torn Africa. England may be a small Island, but our daring people certainly get to the most extreme locations. The English race has acquired much wisdom in the centuries of political wrangling, colonization and world diplomacy. England, I feel is like the wise old man, who's seen it all and is trying to learn by its mistakes, whereas I see America as the young 'pup,' eager and enthusiastic to please, always ready to try something new. America is idealistic about the ease with which it can solve other countries' century old problems and naive in the world's attitude towards itself.

The adventurous spirit is in all British people, we are some of the most travelled people in the world. We are a country whose future is in its past. Our pageantry, castles and history draw the admiration of the world. Even here in Minnesota I have found a large network of British people who band together under the umbrella of an organization called "Daughters of the British Empire." A rather pretentious name that the younger members feel should be changed. This group is found all over the world and is designed to unite British women, offering friendship and support abroad. The first time I attended a meeting, I hadn't seen another British person for over six months and thought I could survive quite easily after eight years in the USA without English companions. But when I walked into the sitting room and heard the chatter of over twenty women talking in the many diverse accents of our British home, I felt an overwhelming sense of relief and comfort. We poured over British newspapers, bid on British candy, jars of jelly and tea bags, in a rather sad auction. We commiserated with older members who had lost loved ones and offered help to the hospitalized or needy.

I looked around the room on that first evening and was amazed at the tenacity of these ladies. Some of them had been here for over thirty years. Their accents hadn't changed; in fact they looked as though they had just 'got off the boat' yesterday. They spoke of how different their experience had been emigrating from Britain. How they couldn't afford to return home and had to wait for fifteen years before they could return to Britain and their loved ones. They talked about the lack of telephones back then and how letters were the only form of communication. They told me how spoilt I was, as I could buy almost all of the foods I missed from England in the local stores here, whereas they had to do without.

When the evening closed and I left in my car, I thought about all these ladies and how different their lives had been to the accepted way of life in Britain. I saw myself sitting at a D.B.E meeting in thirty years' time and wondered if I would still be hankering for British T-bags, Walker's shortbread and a good British newspaper? I felt sad for these stoic women who had travelled so far from home. They seemed lonely to me; they stayed on for their children to have greater opportunities and yet some of their children now live far away in other states. They can't return to Britain, as it's a country that is only familiar in their memories of thirty years ago and most of their British relatives have now passed on.

I love my English friend's eccentricities and value the wisdom they pass on to the younger members like me. They help us navigate the problems of separation, citizenship, aging parents, homesickness and adjustment. They are a perfect example of the British 'stiff upper lip,' they plod on, keeping up appearances, they stick together through life's challenges and are always welcoming to new members.

I am often asked If I am going to stay here in the USA or return to England, and also whether I prefer England to the United States? These are not easy questions, neither do they deserve an 'off the cuff' answer. They are questions that I often ask myself. I look at the puzzle from every angle, it's like a 'Rubik Cube' that slowly falls into place with each passing year of my stay here. I wish I had a crystal ball to resolve this anomaly and give me the resolve to relax, just be here and be myself.

When we first come out to the United States, (or 'Across the pond ' as we like to describe it,) we thought it would be for a year, a business experiment with a safety net to take us home. This was an easy way to cope, just one year, or extended vacation, we kept our home in England and lived in rented accommodation for the duration. There were no risks involved, so we thought. I observed my environment with the aloofness of a tourist, not having to plan ahead or adjust my way of thinking. I felt like I had my nose pressed up against the shop window. I could see in to this country's space, but I didn't have to touch or taste it's permanence.

One of the first phone calls I received in my apartment was from a funeral home, selling cemetery plots, which I was told were selling fast. I replied indignantly that, "I wouldn't be as careless as to die abroad!" and put down the phone. That's how I felt when I first arrived here. That conversation was like a wake up call for me. I had to consider for the first time that I could quite possibly never go home. I was shocked to the core. I imagined my English relatives, years into the future, "Tut-Tutting" in their front parlors, looking at faded photographs of us and recalling that. "Oh yes!, they were the ones that took off to America and didn't come back. I wonder what happened to them?" Will we stare back from those photographs? The All American family, wearing loud t-shirts, baseball caps, with cameras hanging around our necks? Will we be buried in graves in another man's land? I'm not ready to accept that fate yet. My heart still tells me I will return to the land of my birth, to a small, grassy graveyard, in a corner of my distant island home.

Logic tells me that my children are growing up, they look and sound like American kids. Their whole life has been spent in America. They are familiar with its resonance, it is a reality for them and they have no questions in their eyes or sense of their uniqueness in its rhythm. They have no other country that inhabits their dreams and haunts their thoughts. Each year that goes by, I have to release small parts of my English influence on them as they embrace the American world of their school and friends. On the first day of my daughter's kindergarten year, I cried for the loss of my English child. My dreams of an English school, a uniform and the traditions I had grown up with were gone. Now she was leaving my jurisdiction, my little corner of England and she was going to become a 'Gap' kid, ride on the yellow bus to school and be taught to call me 'Mom' instead of 'Mummy' like at home.

Each stage of our life has been a learning experience for all of us and a painful letting go for me. When I hear my little nieces on the phone, I mourn the loss of my children's English accent. When my sister-in-law sends a picture or CD of her children at school or in a concert, I feel a strong nostalgia for the familiar hymns, the school uniforms of my childhood and the sweet cadence of their young English voices.

My experience of parenting has evolved completely in America. I didn't have my family for reassurance and advice. My memories of my own childhood and my mother's parenting techniques have faded, forcing me sometimes to question my own methods. Was I being a bad mother, as I seemed to have a very different outlook on discipline? My expectations for politeness in my children often seemed quaint and too structured compared to my American friends. Uncertainties caused a lack of conviction and confidence in me. Sometimes I longed for my mother to be nearby to help reestablish my English base, in the face of overwhelming Americanism around me.

When my daughter was tiny, she was very active and would never stay close to me. She would wander off and caused quite a few scares when we lost sight of her in stores or at the park. To solve this problem I bought a harness and lead that is designed for toddlers and is commonly used in England, where we tend to walk more frequently, especially near busy roads. I received clear disapproval from fellow shoppers and friends for using it. They seemed to think this was a rather antiquated method, so I soon abandoned the harness, preferring to struggle with my adventurous toddler than feel the wrath of my friends. If my children started to scream in a store, I felt a strong concern from other people who would stare at me, seeming to expect me to solve the problem by, buying the toy, letting the child go home or purchasing the offending candy, The American way seemed to revolve around the child. In England I remember, parents commiserated with each other when a child dissolved into a tantrum in a store, saying "It does get better you know" or "Oh! You poor thing, they drive you mad sometimes don't they?" I remember more of a comradeship amongst the adults, instead of the accusing looks I received here. Maybe it's because I'm the parent now and am much too sensitive? It's hard to judge, as all my parenting has taken place here.

The saying goes that, "We are two countries separated by a common language." This is certainly true, but it is such a subtle translation, it can take years to reveal the layers of tradition and understanding. I find it fascinating to spot the regional differences and link some words to the immigrant's country of descent. Before I came to the United States of America, I divided the American race into, American Indians, African Americans, Mexicans and just "plain old" Americans! Like the cowboys! Of course, now I know better. The diversity in this country is staggering. Just to listen to the roll call at the school is to have a lesson in geography and pronunciation. In my old school, the names were "Good old" English names, Smith, Wood, Shepherd, Brown (This has all changed now) There was no confusion in where these names had come from, Now I'm always interested to ask people where their last name comes from, who were their ancestors and I am amazed at how many have very little clue of their lineage..

I am frequently foiled into thinking that people have understood me or that I have understood them. Their politeness, nodding of heads and glazed expression incorrectly lead me to assume that my order in a restaurant will be correct, that my dry cleaning will come back with light starch, or that my invitation to attend an open house will be accepted at the right time, following the correct directions. But somehow, this isn't so. P.T.O on the bottom of an invitation means, 'please turn over' so my follow on message is not understood and remains unread. The gangly youth in Dairy Queen stares back in disbelief when the sheet cake I attempted to order comes back circular with the wrong message. I have lost count of the times that I have opened my mouth to speak in a store and the cashier has exclaimed, "I just love your accent! Where do you come from?" I forget I am a foreigner. I don't hear my accent and I am often hurt when my bubble of belonging is so easily burst.

I know that my accent is admired and in many ways is an asset. I am effortlessly blessed with a voice that imparts class, wealth, and intelligence. (Gifts that I would truly love to possess.) I feel guilty to benefit from this unwitting subterfuge. Sometimes my accent gets in the way, when a less worldly neighbor assumes that I am in some way related to the Queen, sip high tea with my tiara on, and insist on politeness at all times. Quite a few times I have discovered

I've been nicknamed the Queen behind my back, but I guess there are worse things I could be called, so I'll endure it. It takes a few social gatherings before they realize that the British can be just as bawdy and relaxed as our American counterparts. So I explain this reaction as ... "Waiting for my neighbors to experience the journey." It's a game of patience, which can sometimes prove exhausting when you move a great deal and have to start all over again.

I have found it impossible to blend into the wallpaper at social events, as my accent invariably gives me away, It sometimes puts me at quite a disadvantage, as people always remember me and where they last saw me, but I am not always as quick to remember one American voice amongst many. I think that because of this problem, I tend to just speak up, get my strangeness out of the way and then people can make what they will of me. My English shyness has been shaken off by the necessity of meeting people and trying to build a life here. No one is going to come knocking on our door. My English reserve has been forced to vaporize, as the curious will root me out.

I have been fortunate with the friends that I have made along the way. I rely so heavily on the support of these great people. They share their lives generously and I am always astounded at the hospitality of Americans. Friends have opened their doors to us and included us in their family traditions, celebrations and outings. When I look at the friendships we have made, I see a pattern of friends who have also experienced dramatic moves, life changing events or are foreigners here themselves. We recognize the need in each other and are more open with our hearts and our lives. The bonds of friendships are strong as we invest so much energy and emotion into building a network of family-like ties. Each time we have to move, I have to dig deeper inside myself to find the desire to build, once more, the new friendships and support that we need to survive. I feel like I am betraying my old relationships when I start this process and I've noticed that my reluctance to proceed lasts longer each time. But the incredible people we have met, the life stories we have discovered and become part of, have made the effort worthwhile and greatly enriched our journey.

My English family chides me that I will never return home. They visit us in the United States and marvel at the size of our home, our car and our yard. They enjoy the newness and convenience of the country and the hospitality of the people. They grudgingly understand why we stay here and even admit that perhaps we would be mad to return home. My mother finds it the hardest as we share a special bond. She sometimes feels intimidated by the perfect world of the suburb where we live. When we are invited to my friends' homes, she mocks the squeaky clean houses, that look like nobody lives there. She criticizes the waste of natural resources in our homes and our fuel guzzling cars. She scoffs at the mind numbing TV programs and the enormous plates of food in the restaurants. At these moments, I know how much I have changed. I am no longer intimidated or overwhelmed. My skin has thickened. I am part of this world; it's no longer unreal. I can feel, touch, taste and hear. I am riding in it's current and planning ahead for a future here. I sense my mother's sadness as her days are running out and I still have not returned.

When I last returned to England after a three year break, I felt that I was a foreigner. Although I blend in there, my voice doesn't cause a stir, I'm ignored and no longer special. But I am seeing England as if for the first time like a tourist. The traffic, the crowds, the grating accents of the upper classes and the course shouts of the market boys. This is my country and my people, but I no longer feel one of them. I no longer own a piece of English turf. My old friends have moved on with lives I'm not party to. Family have aged like us, young relatives don't recognize us and I don't relate to personalities on TV or products in commercials. It feels strangely surreal to sit with my family and watch a TV show inhabited by a strange new England that I no longer understand. My memories are stuck back in the England of 1993, as if the clock stuck in time. I am a gypsy, with my past in England, my present in Minnesota and a future that's uncertain in its location.

Whenever we buy a new piece of furniture, I still wonder if it will fit in an English home. When we paint a room, I wonder if it will be neutral enough for the next owner. I dream of a cottage in the Cotswolds in England, with Wellington boots lined up by the door, a garden brimming with perennials, church bells ringing in the distance and mum and I sitting at a pine table with a steaming mug of tea in our hands. My husband tells me to relax and enjoy the present, as the future will work itself out. But I feel like I would be betraying my English heart if I didn't give England at least a backward glance.

Sharp
as a
Knife

Sarah Bromage

Sharp as a Knife

By Sarah Bromage

The Story of Our Canteen
of Cutlery And What a Story!

We have in our possession the most beautiful sterling silver canteen of cutlery, with the initial M on it for my maiden name. My maiden name was Mountain. This canteen was specially commissioned by my grandparents, Nancy and Ken Mountain on my father's side, from Garrard's of London. They are the top silversmiths in England. Anything from there evidently had the extra cachet. This was a gift to my parents on their wedding day in Calcutta, India in 1939 on December 6th. So the canteen had to brave the fierce seas from England to India, but it didn't know it was being brave. My poor grandparents couldn't afford this magnificent gift, but my dear mama was brought up to think you can afford everything and so could everybody else. But, she was only 19! My grandparents had 'only' silver plate themselves, that my mother considered suitable for below stairs. How they found the money I haven't a clue but find it they did.

The canteen is in a large mahogany box that has shown the test of time sadly. Most oddly, there were fourteen main course forks and only nine main course knives and eight dessert spoons and forks, bread knives and fish knives and forks. Tea spoons and coffee spoons and even egg spoons plated in gold to help prevent tarnish. Oh Mama, what were you thinking of!!! The list goes on as to what else this box contains with its beautiful brass insert handles. All these beautiful pieces were used by my parents for dinner parties that my parents gave during the last few years of the British Raj. (Before partition from India and Pakistan) The fans would circulate slowly above the dinner guests as heaven help them if they should dare to feel a sweat. Silver containers were on the table so guests could have a cigarette between courses. Imagine that today in 2019. Then there were the puddings – yes they were called puddings and never desserts or sweets. After the cheese, the men were left to sit and drink port or brandy and mull over men's stuff while my beautiful, elegant Mama withdrew with the ladies to the drawing room and had cigarettes themselves. No wonder she eventually died horribly of COPD. Five years later my father was recalled to London, as it was still World War 2. My mother's main anguish was the sight of her trousseau, including the canteen of silver cutlery, which was in another boat. U boats of course were the worry sailing through the Mediterranean, putting lives at risk not just her trousseau. The canteen was then disembarked at Tilbury docks in London and spent the next few years in an awful wartime flat – no entertaining there. Because of wartime rationing and my birth and my father living elsewhere near the war office for peace and quiet, they stopped all dinner parties.

After that the canteen cheered up as it was sent to the Gold Coast (now Ghana) where it was used for loads of dinner parties. They all knew how to party. Up late in the morning, cocktails, surfing at sea and then drinks and dinner was the normal way of life. My mother never got fat. After that, life got a bit dull as they were posted to Amersham in England at a training college. They had to rent a downstairs flat from a nice woman whose name I can't remember. It was a lovely airy flat; sofas with chintz. What the cutlery did then I am not sure as I do remember my mother being eternally grumpy- hormonal and Daddy having one of his flings. He never could keep it in his trousers!!!

Its next venue was Berlin, in the early 50s, where a lot of entertaining was done. To my mother's joy, they had a maid and a cook. The cook was horrid and we always thought she was an ex-Nazi. Daddy was now a Lieutenant Colonel and had a lot more perks including a chauffeur. I loved it there as a child, being the lazy little tike that I was and still am.

After that, the canteen braved the seas once again and ended up in the centre of Nigeria where it was pressed into use. We had the most amazing cook who only used a wooden stove but cooked the most incredible meals. His onion rings in batter and his treacle tart were mind-blowingly wonderful and remains in my memory today as "the best." He also used to make the most tasty and delicious West African curry lunches on Sundays, so naturally that's what he did every Sunday with endless guests. His curries were legendary. After three years there in hedonistic bliss as there was even someone to clean the silver it was packed up shipped back to the UK. Yet again it travelled over the dangerous seas and on to Norway.

My father was stationed at Kolsas, the NATO headquarters near Oslo. My mother hated Norway. Too much nature and no staff so all the dinner parties were created by her and she also had to clean the silver and do all the dishes or washing up as the English would call it. I know how bored she was as I was too. I had to live there in disgrace after having been expelled from my last school in France. Poor parents had to put up with me. They only had

17

one car between them. I was far too much in love to care though with the healthy Norwegian on my left for just in case and 'the one' in England. There the canteen stayed in Gullhella for two years doing its social bit for NATO and the people Daddy and Mummy had to host. It was witness to a row my father had when I wasn't socially chatty at one of the many dinners when he told me I was being selfish thinking of my shyness and myself. That taught me a lesson much needed and well used to this day. The canteen observed but said nothing.

Then it was packed up and sent to Munchen Gladbach near Dusseldorf, Germany. This was much more fun for the canteen and I was there for loads of dinner parties. My mother, by then, was an amazing cook.

The highlight for the canteen and for me was when it was pressed into action over my wedding celebrations to Christopher. It also viewed Christopher's immediate family not so thrilled about the arrival of myself within their family with my will power and humour and other failings in their eyes. My kind mother laid on a wonderful spread on the night of my wedding for Liv, Biddy and dear Nancy and Granny.

Then it was packed up and sent to Edinburgh where it saw a disastrous dinner party laid on for me when I suddenly had a miscarriage. Daddy thought I had done it on purpose, but the canteen witnessed my voice saying I had been stuck in the back of his car for twenty hours driving back and forth to Mull with them both smoking. I had an answer for everything. However, it was a relief as Mel was only 10 months old. Then the canteen was sent via truck and sea to the Isle of Mull and dear lovely Oak Bank. (I wish the house had been on the mainland and then I would have kept it.)

When my parents died Christopher, I with Jonathan, gave a dinner party for Clive and Marjorie using what was left of the rest of the canteen as Daddy had given what I could carry on the train home to Devon for a party for our silver wedding.

However the evident social life of the canteen of cutlery had its apex when Prince William of Gloucester and his girlfriend came to stay in the 1970s before he was killed in a plane crash. Prince William came to stay three times and by the third visit the canteen and my parents had had enough of royalty for the time being. It was used for breakfast, lunch and dinner. This was unheard of in its history as none of us eat breakfast and not in a state of grandeur in the dining room with the silver in use. It I am sure was exhausted. We always had plenty of salmon due to my father's housekeeper Chrissie who had connections with a local salmon farm. The fish set was often in use thanks to her. We were never allowed to enquire as to where it came from!!!!!

After my father died and Oak Bank sadly was sold, the canteen or what was left of it was packed up with everything else and transported to Paddocks Cottage in Devon. Christopher and I had lived there by then for over thirty years. The canteen was reunited with the rest of itself where it was used frequently for dinner parties. I admit to not looking after it that well at the time with rather useless excuses. I also had what I grandly called my "kitchen silver." This was the cutlery that had daily use. Whenever I had little gifts of money I would go to antique shops and buy an antique fork or dessert spoon. Christopher gave me a collection of Georgian coffee spoons for Christmas.

Everything is still in use here in Minnesota. For reasons that I won't enter into now we decided to move to Minnesota in the USA and the canteen and I had to look up in our atlas where in the USA that was. Three months after we arrived in Minnesota the canteen and all our other possessions took up residence in our home in the Twin Cities. Today it is very well cared for and is all complete next to the dining table.

After 80 years the canteen has come to a halt for the moment until it moves onto the next member of the family who I hope will enjoy it.

I Just Washed My Jeans

and Can't Do a Thing in Them

Marj Helmer

I Just Washed My Jeans and Can't Do a Thing in Them

By Marj Helmer

Ugh! I guess I'll have to lie on the bed to zip up. Happens every time I wash these jeans. And I didn't even put them in the dryer. I know better. They hang at least a day in the laundry room. Getting in my way and falling down all the time. And they need washing, although I think some people never do wash their jeans.

There! I zipped and buttoned up. Now I just have to get up. Roll over. Slide to the edge of the bed. Feet on the floor. Push up. There! Ready for the day. Oops! I forgot to put my socks on. I'll never reach my feet now. So, sandals? No, there's snow out there. Well then, sneakers without socks. Who can tell? The jeans will pull up when I sit down. But I won't be doing much of that today.

I can sit down in my jeans, but if I sit too long, I develop acid reflux. Even if I don't eat or drink, there's an uprising in my throat. If I'm in the car, I can open the waist, like a middle aged man I saw, who quick zipped up when he got out of his car. Or maybe he was a flasher. However, in the coffee shop, with or without friends, I won't be unzipping.

23

I hope I don't drop anything. Besides displaying "plumber's butt," I can't bend at the knees in my jeans, much less at the waist. So then there's that spread eagle stance with my rear in the air while I grope on the floor, bobbing up and down, trying to trap what I dropped. If I have to actually get down, I need to crawl to a chair and hoist myself up, or try that four point position and jack upright in a minimum of two attempts. A super sloppy "downward facing dog." You don't want to see it.

Hugging little kids is also a stretch. It's better if I lift them, but the bigger ones I have to bend down to hug. And I couldn't not hug. I live for hugs. With significant others, jeans are a big plus. They present a very firm bum to pat. Yes, sir!

They're warm that's for sure. But then what about the summer? Of course, I could ventilate them. Strategic holes and rips, not to be sexy, but to be cool. Oh wait, that could mean sexy too. You know what I mean.

There's also the question of the top. You need an oversized sweater or shirt to hide the midriff bubbling up above the waistline like a "muffin top." Don't even think of tucking in. And a belt just accentuates the problem.

But it's the fashion, isn't it? Everyone wears jeans. For everything. Just add the proper accessories. It's certainly better than polyester slacks with elastic waists or those "Mom Jeans" from Saturday Night Live.

I don't look that bad, do I? And besides, tomorrow they'll be looser again.

Biting My Tongue

at the Dog Park

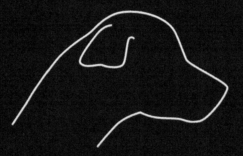

Mary Mitchell Lundeen

Biting My Tongue at the Dog Park

By Mary Mitchell Lundeen

The sun was low in the sky as I arrived at the dog park. Spring weather brought many of us out of our cocoons and back into our warmer weather routines.

"Hi Debbie, it is so great to see you!" I shouted and smiled broadly as I opened the gate. Debbie was one of the regulars at the dog park and she had not been here in many months. "Long time no see!" I shouted in her general direction as I unleashed my dog to let him join the sniffing and peeing and running. This was a place where the dogs could follow their basic instincts. It was also a place where the community came together. It was good to see Debbie and reconnect with her since she had her firstborn last fall. She and her husband were so excited to be parents and had definite plans about how they were going to raise their children. Debbie was going to be a stay at home Mom in order to carry out these plans. "So, this is your baby. I am very excited to meet him" I said as I moved closer to Debbie and the stroller. I leaned in to get a peek. The baby was watching the dogs running past in a pack. "What is his name?"

"Colin." replied Debbie. The baby was squirming and

looked like he wanted to move.

"Can I hold him?" I asked. Babies at this age did not like to stay still.

"Sure, he has been in the stroller for a while. I had to make sure the dogs were OK. We just got here" said Debbie. Debbie unhooked the little guy, picked him up and handed him to me. There were two other women with their dogs that I recognized from previous trips to the dog park. I said hello to them and smiled while I moved with Colin to sit down at the nearby picnic table.

I sat down and held little Colin facing me. "Well hello there big guy," I said with enthusiasm. I gave him a big smile expecting a goofy, drool filled, overstretched smile in return. He felt stiff in my arms. Colin focused his gaze at my necklace and reached a chubby hand clumsily towards it. Oh no. "You see my necklace" I commented. I let him grab and touch the circular metal with a nickel sized blue stone inside. "You like my necklace. You are such a big boy". Colin looked from my necklace to my mouth. "Hi buddy boy" I said in response to this. His eyes remained locked right to my mouth movements. Shit, shit, shit.

As one of the big dogs ran close to us, Colin shifted his gaze and tracked the dog for a few seconds and then focused back to the necklace. As another couple of dogs ran past, I said loudly, "Oh look the puppy dogs" and turned my head in an exaggerated fashion. Nothing. No attempt to look. Colin was still grabbing my necklace. This is bad. Debbie, who had been talking to the other women, came walking over.

"Here's your little guy" I said quietly as I handed him back to her.

Colin settled into a familiar position with his mother. He had his arms outstretched and was rotating his wrists. He leaned back as far as he could from her embrace. Looking past his mother's face to the lawn, Colin was making a crying ahh ahh noise with varying degrees of intensity. Debbie first presented the Tupperware of Cheerios and then, when Colin did not reach for those, a pacifier was put near his mouth. This too was not taken. He continued to make the noise and rotate his wrists. Debbie began a rhythmic rocking motion as Colin's chanting continued. Enough, this was much too painful, I had to walk away.

I passed by the stroller a couple of times over the next few minutes as I played with the dogs. I overheard a few nuggets of information that Debbie was sharing with the other women......Colin was now 11 months old; just started crawling; he had been a hard, fussy baby; and it has been a long year for Debbie.

I could have written that script after holding him for two minutes. This baby has some degree of Autism, which is not obvious to everyone yet. But obvious to me. Does he smile? Yes, the parents can get a smile when they do a repetitive physical action, but this is not good enough; not the quality that should be seen. Colin's lack of interest in faces was classic. I felt sick to my stomach. I have been part of many

29

parents slowly discovering the fact that their child has a social disability. This nice young couple has a very rough road ahead. They think he is perfect, just fussy. He does some of the basic developmental milestones every once in a while. It is just enough to keep them believing nothing is wrong. But It is not enough. Not nearly enough in quantity or quality.

The dog park is a place for basic instincts and for making connections. Pooping, peeing, making conversation or, on this day, perceiving an upcoming train wreck. I walked over to the fence and picked up my dog's poop in a plastic bag ...crap, shit...words so very appropriate for my feelings at this moment in time.

Winter

Caroline Munro

Winter

By Caroline Munro

Snow falling on snow, wind blowing, dancing snowflakes, side winding waves of crystals gusting into snow crevices of tree bark, balling like frozen fists into the shadow of bushes, probing into corners of the deck and house, showering lawn furniture with a cover of sparkling dust. Nature spray paints the dark striations of the wooden deck, each board marked with winters chalk. Parallel lines, man-made dimensions, softened with a frosted lip. Steps soundproofed with a cushion of snow. Gate swinging hard in the gusting ice squall, thudding wood against wood, each blow throwing a whirling dervish of snow from wood to air, where it's whisked away to settle on bush or grass. Mother Nature, dissatisfied with her work, rearranges at her will and, impatient with the results, continues to transform the objects of her wrath.

Icicles hang from roof and gutter, glass splinters attached by winters mighty will to man's structure, deforming our linear rooflines with crystal tassels, shining fringes and snowy braid. Each window dusted with a cobweb of ice diamonds, giving a softly focused view from each window lens. Winter mocks our love of order, straight lines and balance, showering us with soft snow and hard ice that misguides angles, distorts shapes, swamps the unsightly and emphasizes winter's beauty.

The softly falling snow insulates the house, only the wind whistles around the corners of the unrelenting brick and howls down the chimney to warn of winter's fury outside. The icy wind ebbs and flows like a great freezing ocean. Silence builds until a crescendo of air buffets the house and rattles the windows, a throb of wind sucks the air up into the sky and then hurls it back at man's defenses. We hold our breath and wait for the house to be unhinged and spun into the elements. But Winter likes to tease us, like a cat playing with a mouse, once the head is off, the cat loses interest and so too does winter, moving on to greater sport in another man's backyard.

The stormy seas of winter winds, ebb and flow, quiet once again, descends upon the house. The snow settles into a desert landscape, devoid of recognizable landmarks. Plants enveloped with snow dunes throw up small flag markers to show where a perennial once stood. Trees and bushes look like an exercise in light and dark, the snow having been blasted to one side of all standing things. The creek is now indistinguishable from the lawn, only the iced grass, bent over with the weight of snow, delineates the two. The snow cover is perfect and spotless, no footprint or blemish spoils the purity of this white, silent world. No bird sings or animal ventures out, all is calm after the storm.

The Trusted

Killer

Lise Spence-Parsons

The Trusted Killer

By Lise Spence-Parsons

The phone rang and rang on the desk. In fact, it was one of many phones all ringing on the desks in the large white-walled room. There were lots of people answering the phones, but they still rang. Loud shrill rings, shouting out "answer me, answer me....me me me."

He stood in the middle of the room, staring out towards the window, but not really seeing the outside. He felt odd, confused by the facts that were being presented to him from all angles. He swiveled his head towards the bank of white boards, and saw the montage of women's faces stuck to the board in what looked like a random pattern, but was in fact the order of their respective murders, or at least when they were found. They spanned from June 2011 to November 2016. There had been no more bodies found for two years now, but that did not indicate that the murders had stopped, merely that the murderer or murderers were getting more accomplished in body disposal. He turned his head a little more to the right to a second bank of boards, this was sparser in its accumulation of evidence. It was the board of possible suspects. Most had been crossed off now, as having an alibi. The third set of information on the last board was simply a time line of murders in a linear form. Some detectives found that a more helpful approach.

So here they all were, had been in fact, since January 2017, taking phone leads from the public and following up on them all. Most, of course, turned out to be useless, at best people were misinformed, at worst they aimed to mislead. He couldn't count the number of false starts they had over the last couple of years. It was exhausting, but he was determined to find the murderer of these innocent young women.

The women, had some commonality, they were all younger than 30. They had all disappeared after an evening out on the town. They all had no serious boyfriend or partner. However, other than that, they were unique, worked in different industries, came from different economic, social and religious backgrounds, lived in different areas, and had no common appearance. There was one medical connection they all had, and it may not have been even known to them; they were all at least eight weeks pregnant at time of their murders. They had interviewed all the women's doctors and other medical assistants to find a common thread tying them together, but to no avail. It was mystifying to him, but he would not give up.

He looked at his watch. It was 11 am on Tuesday and the phones were going crazy. He could overhear snippets of one-sided conversations, confirming times, dates, places, descriptions. It was a never ending task. It was a painstaking exercise in what appeared to be futility. He been called to the Police Commissioner's office the previous month, to share what information they had so far with the powers that be. They'd decided to share some more information with the press by releasing the pregnancy information to the public, but not in its entirety, it was far too barbaric. So far, they'd kept a lot of the more gorier details secret for the fear of copy-cat murderers starting another spree. He was scheduled to go on national TV this afternoon and then brief the press directly afterwards to catch that evening's papers.

They had debated for weeks on whether to take this step. He was still unsure, but the investigation was getting nowhere fast. Someone, somewhere, knew this murderer, a he or she, they had not ruled out a female assailant who was some was someone's child, partner, spouse, co-worker. All they really had to go on was the knife was wielded by a left-handed person, who had great upper body strength. The police also had surmised that it was probably a person known to them first hand or a very close connection, as none of the bodies bore that many self-defense marks.

He turned again to the window and stared into space, the sounds of the room dimming, as he played the names of the nine women through this mind in order; Susan, Anne, Claire, Amy, Samantha, Diana, Tara, Marsha and Denise, god what a waste.

"Sir, Inspector Cline, do you have a moment?" He spun on his heel and responded the uniform police constable,

"Yes, Constable, errr, Piper, what can I help you with?"

"Sorry Sir, we just got a call, they found another body, down by the canal!"

"Oh god. Okay, come on, let's get down there. Damon, grab the team and SOCO and let's move it! Thanks, Piper for the update, can you get a message to the Press Office, that I will have to delay the press release?"

"Yes Sir, no problem."

The Inspector and his plain clothes detectives jumped into three cars that were outside the incident room and sped away to the canal.

Upon reaching the canal, and navigating through the closed roads and yellow tape, the team got to the canal. They suited up and were directed to a houseboat sitting at the side of the canal at the lock gates.

"So, what have we got Doc?" He addressed his question to the overworked medical examiner.

"Female, approximately 27 years of age, no ID, sexually assaulted, belly slashed and uterus cut," the ME looked pale and nauseous, although this was his job, it did not get any easier. "We will know more in a few hours, I will push this ahead at the morgue."

"Thanks Doc, any rough idea of time of death?"

"Hard to say, but rigor has not set in yet, so I'd say around eight or nine this morning."

"Wow, they're getting brave, broad daylight at the lock gates in a busy area in rush hour!"

"Brave or stupid Inspector!"

Just then Damon walked up. "Found this Guv, in the barge." He handed the Inspector a small scrap of paper with what looked like a partial phone number. "One of the techs said she been holding it in her hand when they first arrived."

"Bag it, Damon, and get some photos for our info board."

"Yes Guv," Damon went back onto the barge and he heard him telling someone else to get a photo or two.

"Damon, I'm off back to the station. Send Sheila back up would you? She can drive me back. I'd better brief the big wigs upstairs!"

Yes, Guv." Sheila re-appeared from down below in the barge and they left the scene to SOCO and the ME team.

The Inspector went to see his boss, the Police Commissioner on the 5th floor and spent about an hour sharing the latest news.

"I think we should delay the press release Sir. It might do more harm than good. I'm waiting for forensics and I do have the partial phone number to work on. It could be the breakthrough we are waiting for!"

"Ok, I'm off the same mind Cline. You have a week, to pull something out of the bag, but then we need to go public. I'm getting pressured by the Prime Minister's office all the time, they want results!"

"I understand, Sir." He stood to return back to the incident room.

"Thank you Cline, for all your and your team's hard work. I couldn't have a better officer in charge. Let's get this done and then bloody celebrate!"

"Yes Sir. Thank you Sir."

Back in the incident room, someone had added the Jane Doe photos to the board, added dates, and locations, and updated the time line. The scrap of paper was bagged and safely put away in the evidence room, but an image of the number had been shared with all concerned.

"Ok listen up all," Cline called out to the room, "you have the partial phone number. We need to get this matched to a person or at least a place. Limit the radius to ten miles. Do a phone search and then start calling."

"That could be thousands of calls Sir!"

"Yes, well then you'd better get started!" He snapped at the unlucky foot soldier who had dared to voice the obvious. "Once I get a forensic report from the ME, we may be able to narrow it down a little."

He went back into his office, closed the door, and sat with his head in his hands. It was two years, ten women all killed in the same way and no closer to solving it. This person, no sub-human, was having a laugh at their expense. Cline's cell phone rang.

"Yes, ok, yes, so the same MO, great. She was pregnant, nine weeks or so. Ok, well thanks for calling, if you could match dental records to give us a name. Tomorrow? Great... thanks. Bye."

He hung up and then stared at the phone, the number that called still visible on the screen, 563 2154, it looked remarkably similar to the scrap of paper the Jane Doe was holding. He ran back into the main office.

"Hold up, what is the number you have on the paper, anyone?"

"563 21 Sir."

"Is Damon back?"

Yes Sir. He's in the canteen, feeding his face."

The Inspector almost ran from the room and down to the canteen, "Damon, quick, get the team, we are going to the hospital."

"Guv?"

"I think our murderer works there. The phone number is a partial match."

Again three cars left the station, this time towards the hospital pre natal wing. They turned into the car park, and made their way inside. Cline indicated to two of his team to block the exit, whilst the rest spanned out into the corridors going off to various treatment rooms. The Inspector and Damon approached the reception desk, showed their warrant cards and asked to see the records of the nine known murdered women. The assistant stalled, not knowing if she could share the medical records.

"I have a warrant on its way, Miss Brown," the Inspector stated reading the hapless girl's badge. "It's absolutely paramount that we see these records right now in a private room."

Sally, nodded and went to fetch the paper records. She returned within 5 minutes holding a stack of files and indicated a room to her left. Just then, one his team arrived holding the warrant. "There you go Sally. All is in order. Okay I'm leaving my men on the exit. Are there any other exits from this unit?"

"Yes, one down the end there, the Emergency Exit."

"Ok thanks," he directed two of his team to that door. He and the other five detectives went into the room and started scanning the files.

All were laid out the same manner, name, address, date of birth, date of conception and projected birth date. Under that, the attending doctors and clinical assistants were listed. They began to call out names and dates, and suddenly one name kept appearing on all the records, a Dr. M. Greene, a pregnancy specialist in high risk cases. The doctor was listed as practicing here in the pre natal one day a week and other units on other days. Cline's cell phone started to ring, he jumped and answered.

"Cline here, Yes? You have a name of our Jane Doe?" He waved his arm at Damon and indicated for him to write this down. "Penelope Calder, 26, ten weeks pregnant approximately."

He finished up the call. "Get that file Sheila please. I have a feeling our Dr. Greene will be listed!"

"Yes Sir." She returned with the file and to no one's amazement, yes, Dr. M. Greene was listed as providing a consult two weeks ago.

The Inspector got copies of the relevant parts of the files, gave them back to Sally with instructions to keep them in a secure place. Then he asked her if Dr. Greene were around

43

today?

"No, Inspector, not today, she works at Charing Cross Hospital today until 6 pm." Cline glanced at his watch, 4:30 pm. It was rush hour and on the other side of town. "Quick to the cars, we need to get to Charing Cross. Someone call ahead for uniform back up, we have an arrest to make."

With sirens blaring and lights flashing the team crossed London as quickly as possible and were met by a team of uniforms from the local station. They located the pre natal unit and went straight in, and using the same warrant, asked a bored looking receptionist, for the whereabouts of Dr. Greene.

"She's in the delivery room with an expectant mother, you can't go in there!"

"Sorry love, but we are!" You two stay here in case she tries to run."

The Inspector and his team went down the corridor to the delivery room and just as they approached, the door opened and a tall, attractive, mid 30's doctor in a white coat came out.

"Dr. Greene?"

"Yes, can I help you?"

"You are under arrest for the murder of ten pregnant women. Damon read the good doctor her rights!"

The
Invitation

Sybil Swanson

The Invitation

By Sybil Swanson

THE MORNING

A day hardly gets any more beautiful than it is this morning. Here I am having a yummy latte at my favorite coffee shop gazing up at the gorgeous cerulean blue sky with big, white, billowy clouds. I sip my latte and lose myself in my new book. Everything seems perfect until suddenly I am accosted. Yes, accosted by this stranger. Well, I must admit a very handsome stranger, but a stranger no less. I say accosted because he is poking my shoulder and practically yelling at me.

"Sophie, Sophie Stevens, what are you so interested in reading?"

"What? What?" I ask, startled as I come back from the fantasy I am reading. "Oh! Oh, I'm sorry. You seem to know my name, but I don't believe I know you. How may I help you?"

"Finally. I have had an incredibly hard time locating you, but I have found you just in time. I am here to invite you to a special gala. Something I am sure you will enjoy." he replied.

"Oh no." I answer.

"But oh yes", he said.

"I couldn't possibly go. I'm too busy. But wait, when is this gala?"

"It is this evening. I apologize for the late notice, but as I said, I've had a very difficult time finding you. However, all the necessary details are noted on the invitation. All you do is show up and enjoy yourself. It's a special night so I suggest you wear your finest. And, oh yes, please wear your hair long as you look so lovely when you do. See you later."

"Wait, wait!" What the heck just happened? A complete stranger just hands me an invite and then walks away without any explanation or even introducing himself. I don't know that guy, but I'd certainly like to. Definitely the tall, dark and handsome prince of any fairytale. Somebody must be playing a joke on me, but who would do that? What does he mean, wear my hair long; how does he know what I look like with my hair down, much less his liking it that way. I've never seen him before. I'd definitely remember meeting that hunk. Well, I hope I do see him again; I have a lot of questions for him, plus he's great to look at and I love his deep, resonate voice.

THE AFTERNOON

I think I've read this invitation a hundred times and still don't know anything other than I am one of a select group who has been invited to a formal gala at an address I'm not familiar with, tonight at 7:00 PM sharp. This is silly, I'm sure it's a joke. But what if it isn't and I'd be passing up a great opportunity to hobnob with the rich and famous. Yah, who else goes to "galas"? No, it must be a joke. I'm not going to this gala. However, no one has called me today and fessed up to playing a joke on me.

I definitely cannot go to this party, rather "gala". I don't have anything to wear. My "finest" he said. Heck, I'm a jeans and t-shirt kind of gal. Wait! Wait. I remember receiving a huge box of stuff from my Aunt Kate. I was just too sad after she passed away, so never went through it. She was always dressed to the nines and going to parties. Maybe there's something special in the box that I could wear.

Well, I've found the box, but nothing. Nothing. What's this? Oh, there's a box within a box. Maybe this is what I need. Wow! Well, Aunt Kate, I think you knew something I didn't. I now have something special to wear. Very special. That is, if I were going to this shindig, which I'm not! But, if I were, this would be perfectly wonderful to wear. Hmmmm. Maybe I should go. What a shame to leave that gorgeous, sexy dress in the box.

LATE AFTERNOON

I think I'll listen to my favorite talk show while I'm getting ready. Hmmm. Lucky me, I'm having a good-hair day. No frizz. Perfect. Oh my gosh, oh, it's him on the radio! I'd know that voice anywhere. He's talking about the different types of galas going on throughout the city this very night. All different types: Regency parties, costume parties, wine tasting parties, childhood friend parties, remembrance parties, writing parties, painting parties and on and on. Whatever for? Should I go, should I not go? Is it dangerous? Is it fate? I don't know what to do. I'm in such a tizzy. If I don't go, I will be sitting at home by myself, as usual, regretting that I didn't go. If I do go, I'll at least find out why all these parties. I might really have a blast, meet new people, who I might even like. Or not. At least I know it isn't a joke being pulled on me. Oh, what to do.

Here I've gotten myself ready and still not sure I'm going. All I have left to do is to slip on that to-die-for dress. Thank you, Aunt Kate. I'm so glad I'm the same size as you were. Okay. Decision made. I'm going. Better call Uber quickly.

THE EVENING

Dang, Uber hasn't responded yet and it's getting late. I'll just try to hail a cab at the corner. If I can't get one, then that will mean I'm not supposed to go.

What's this? A limo with my name on the card? Wow! This is amazing! I'm definitely going now.

This can't be a joke. No jokester I know would go to the expense of hiring a limo. I guess I'm going in full bore now and will believe in fairy tales and prince charming for the night. I think I now know how Cinderella felt. I'm rather excited in finding out how all this turns out. Who cares why.

Here we are pulling into the yacht club. No wonder I didn't recognize the address. I guess I'm sailing this evening. Time to chill, Sophie, time to let life happen instead of playing it safe all the time.

I am walking slowly across the gangplank onto the most beautiful and sleek seafaring yacht I've ever laid eyes on. Okay. I haven't seen many yachts, but this is obviously the most beautiful because it's me going aboard. I'm really excited but scared too. I'm definitely not in familiar territory, by a long shot.

I've now walked the gangplank and nothing untoward has happened. Yet. Oh, my goodness! Here comes the most handsome man, a very well-built man, directly towards me. Am I dreaming? No...I know who he is. I just don't know his name...yet.

"Welcome aboard, Sophie. You look...you look absolutely stunning. Red sequins become you. I'm delighted you're here and that you took the invite and the instructions seriously. Thank you for trusting me", he said.

"You are most welcome, sir. However, you keep calling me by name, but I have no name for you."

50

"Please forgive my manners, Sophie. I am Rob. You may go to the area straight ahead and have a refreshment. Everything is on the house this evening so enjoy yourself. And, Sophie", he continued as he gently turned me to look directly into his ice-blue eyes, "keep a space, a very large space on your dance card for me later this evening. Now go and introduce yourself to your new friends. I must attend to my duties."

"Thank you, Rob. I definitely want to have a few minutes of your time as I have a few questions for you, so at your request, I will save a space for you on my dance card." I smile and quickly walk away. Wow! I'm not sure what just happened to me but when he looked at me with his beautiful eyes, he seemed to pierce my very soul. Be still my heart!

I quickly gaze around the room and see a group of women chatting amiably in the far corner where there is a great view of the coastline. The city lights seem to twinkle in the twilight. As I'm puzzling what to do next a glamorous, tall, redheaded woman walks toward me. "Hi", she said in this sexy Marilyn Monroe voice. "I'm Serena and would love to have you join me and the other ladies over in the corner."

"Hi, I'm Sophie. Thanks, I'd love to join you. I feel a little lost not knowing anyone."

"Don't worry, none of us knew each other an hour ago. Just come on and meet everyone. I believe you're the last one to be joining our group. Hey, everyone, this is Sophie. She's the lady we've been waiting for to make us an even dozen. Go ahead and introduce yourselves."

"So nice to meet all of you. What's going on? I'm in the dark here. All I know is that I was to show up by 7 PM, in my finest. I think I got the "finest" right, but I'm a little late."

"Well, Sophie, you know what we know. And, yes, you did get the "finest" right. Serena seems to have a few more details. Please tell us what you know, Serena", requested Scarlet.

"We obviously were to arrive here in our finest, meet each other, have drinks and appetizers for starters, during which time we are to hear from the handsome gentleman who greeted us as to the agenda for the rest of the evening. I admit to having a peek around as I was the first of us to arrive, and what I found is there are several very fine gentlemen next door with whom we are to meet. Now that is what I surmise, and I certainly hope it's true, because they are very handsome men. Right out of *GQ*."

"So, this is all it is, a dating match? I can do that on-line. As nice as it is, I don't need all this glam to get a date. However, I must admit, I'm pretty certain I wouldn't meet that handsome greeter on-line!"

"Sophie, I think most of us feel that way, but I believe there's more to it than that. Unfortunately, I don't know what", replied Serena. "I do know there will be a band and dancing on the upper deck later and that we'll be having a lovely dinner, with dessert, which, of course, includes chocolate. Always a favorite, right? There is one other thing I know and that is the fact that there are some wonderful appetizers next door and we should get ourselves over there before the guys eat them all up. Come on, let's go, Ladies!"

Laid before us is shrimp cocktail with shrimp the size of small lobsters, asparagus tips with capers and pine nuts, shrimp-filled artichokes with mustard dressing, asparagus with orange hollandaise dipping sauce, shrimp and scallops with mixed herbs, bruschetta and other items I've never heard of before. Plus, a wine and champagne tasting bar. Life hardly gets any better than this!

"These appetizers are absolutely scrumptious! What's your favorite, Samantha?

"I'm loving these shrimp-filled artichokes. Absolutely divine; however, if I take one more bite, I won't be able to eat anything at dinner. I see you are having a love affair with the shrimp and scallops!"

"And the champagne! I'm sure if I went shopping for it, I'd come out of the shop empty handed, feeling like a pauper. This is the finest I've ever had. I can't begin to think how much it is a bottle."

"Oh, Sophie, you don't recognize Dom Perignon?"

"This is Dom Perignon? Samantha, I've never had Dom Perignon. No wonder I'm loving it. I don't have occasion to hobnob as we are tonight. Obviously, you are more familiar to this lifestyle than I."

"Some of us here tonight are models, so, yes, I do get to hobnob, as you say, and am familiar with wonderful wines and champagnes like this. Once, I almost had the opportunity to win a bottle of the legendary 1996 Dom Perignon Rose Gold Methuselah. I say 'almost' because it was a drawing and my ticket number was but two numbers off from the winner's ticket. I found out later that a bottle of that champagne costs about $49,000."

"O-M-G! Forty-nine thousand dollars? No way, Samantha. That would be such a waste on me. However, I could quickly get used to having this lovely champagne."

"Don't fall too hard, Sophie. I saw the bottle, and that is a 2005 Moet & Chandon Dom Perignon which runs only about $170 a bottle. A mere pittance by comparison!"

"Ok, ladies, everything I'm experiencing tonight is out of my league. Is there no one else who would be joining me in the pauper's room?"

"Oh, yes, I would be joining you, Sophie," said Sceone.

"Me too," whispered Suzanna.

"No, you're not alone, Sophie, I too would join you in that room," admitted Scarlett.

"Thank you, ladies. I was afraid I am the only pauper here tonight and that I really am Cinderella. I must add though, that every one of us look stunning, glamorous and very wealthy this evening. I also have a tidbit to add to solving the mystery of this evening...I know the name of the handsome man who greeted us."

"AAAAAH! Do tell immediately, or we will have you walk the gangplank", promised Saundra as everyone laughed.

"If you would all quiet down, and stop laughing, I will tell you. However, I think you should let him introduce himself on his own. I don't know his last name...yet, but he did tell me his name is Rob. And he's mine, ladies!"

"Now, Sophie, don't be greedy, it's better to share."

"Oh, Sarah, I might share if he was someone else, but I get these vibes that we've known each other before, and we are a couple. Or will be soon. Very soon. Oh, here he is now."

"Ladies and Gentlemen. I am Rob, your greeter and MC this evening. The handsome dudes you see behind me were college mates of mine. One evening, at one of our own personal reunions, we discovered we all had a similar story. We each remembered someone from our childhood whom we wanted to get to know better but either didn't have enough time to do so, or we were such clueless dorks and too shy to even talk to the girl, or at least get her phone number. So, each of you became the girl left behind by one of these gentlemen here tonight. You, my dear ladies, are the childhood sweethearts we all dreamed of marrying some day! Well, at least to get a date with! Tonight, we get to find out happened to that girl, or guy, you met when you were younger. Some of us had an easy time locating you, and some of us had great difficulty, but we all eventually succeeded. In various forms, this type of gala is happening throughout the city tonight. So, let me introduce you. Rather, I should say, re-introduce you."

"After you all have been re-introduced, we'll adjourn to the dining room and have a virtual feast during which you'll be able to get re-acquainted. Then we'll gather on the top deck to dance under the stars this beautiful evening. I'll start off with you, Serena, since you were the first to arrive. Serena, let me re-introduce you to Rourke Ritter whom you met at a beach when you were 16."

"Rourke? But you were so skinny! Wow! You obviously have been working out since then," said Serena. "Oh, I'm so sorry for my lack of manners. I'm just so surprised and very delighted to meet you again, Rourke."

"I would say that you too have changed quite a bit, Serna", replied Rourke. "I'm really anxious to hear what's been happening in your life, but I suppose we should first step off to the side so the next lucky couple can get re-introduced."

"Phew. Well, the first re-intro went well, let's continue to see how the rest go", said Rob. "Next is ..."

"Obviously the last re-introduction is me, Rob, aka Robbie Roman to the lovely and vivacious, Sophie Stevens."

"You? You are little Robbie? Robbie from the Lake Ottawa Lodge Resort?"

"Yes, the one and the same, Sophie."

"Oh my. How did you ever find me? I can't believe this! I must be dreaming. There's no way you could find me after all the moves my family made. What are you, a private detective?"

"No, not a private detective by trade, but I frequently felt like one trying to track you down", Rob chuckled. "Come, let's go to the dining room and we can catch up there, Sophie.

"I have to admit it took me the longest time to find my long-lost lady but find you I did. Just in time. I thought I was going to be dateless tonight, but there you were this morning, so engrossed in your book. I am more than delighted you came. I wasn't sure you would."

"I have to admit I almost didn't come, Rob. But fortunately, I finally made the decision to do so. I am finding this evening to be incredible. Even more incredible that it's you, little Robbie, sitting here. Hard to believe you are him. I remember you thought I was a lot older than you, but I was just taller. You were so cute, now so handsome. I believe you have grown an inch or two since that summer at the resort. What a thrill to meet you again."

"How did you, all of you, ever accomplish finding us after all these years? I must have moved a dozen times. I did write, as I promised, but I didn't send the letter. I was only 12 and had no stamps and then suddenly we were moving. I lost the letter and your address. It was wild and crazy times. Then we moved again, then again, and then I lost count. And before you ask, no, dad wasn't in the service and we weren't army brats. Maybe brats at times, between my brother and I, but not military. I did get the impression moving all the time was about dad's line of work, but I never found out because both my parents died in a fatal car crash. Then my Aunt Kate took my brother, Sam and I in. About a year later Sam was caught with a gang member immediately following a high-profile robbery. It was assumed, and never proven otherwise, that my brother was part of the gang and part of the robbery, so he was sent to jail along with the other gang members. Sam was released about a year ago, but that didn't last long. He is currently being held without bail for a smuggling scheme that has been in all the papers. You probably saw it and know the rest of the story. Is that how you found me?"

"Before you answer that and you tell me what you've been doing all these years, Rob, I have to ask, when did you ever see me with my hair long?"

Huh? What? Oh, darn, I hate alarms. Especially hate it when they wake me in the middle of a dream. A great dream too. Wow, it seemed so real. I can hardly bring myself back to the real world. Hmmmm, maybe this dream is telling me something; maybe telling me I should try to find this guy named Rob. Maybe, maybe that's it! Yes, I'm going to do it, I'm going to try to find this Rob guy. Rob, Robbie. Do I remember ever meeting a Rob? Yah, at a resort years ago. He was such a cutie and I'll bet he did become a very handsome man. Of course, I don't know if he's taken, but there's only one way to find out. Now what was his last name? Could it really have been Roman, like in the dream? Impossible. But as I think about it, I really think his name was Robbie Roman. I'll need help with this challenge. Maybe Lisa and Carol will help me; they love a mystery.

"Hi, Lisa, hold on while I get Carol on the call too. Carol? Lisa? You both on the line? I just had to call you two to tell you all about my absolutely incredible dream last night. Yes, there is a man in the picture. But the reason I'm calling you is because I need your help. You both will love this."

Inattention
Blindness

Carolyn Wilhelm

Inattention Blindness

By Carolyn Wilhelm

"Why can't I talk on my cell phone when I'm driving?" she whined.

"You are looking at this all wrong," he said.

"I call 'em like I see 'em," she said.

"You need a new perspective, that's for sure! Watch this video and count the number of times the basketball bounces on the floor."

"OK. I am looking right at the video, see?"

"Sigh, I wish you would think while watching the video clip."

"I see basketball players bouncing a ball. I counted eight ball bounces; it is clear as day."

"Rewind the video and really look. You are missing something big!"

"Big? How can that be? This time I counted ten ball bounces. Is that better?"

"Quit counting, and watch it once again, please," he demanded.

"Oh! My! There is a gorilla in the video plain as day! I see it now," she said thankfully. "How did I miss that?"

"Sometimes you can't see the forest for the trees, or maybe the gorilla for keeping your eye on the ball," he laughed. "Inattention blindness happens to the best of us."

"OK, I get it! I shouldn't talk on my cell phone and drive anymore!"

"Bingo!"

Magic
Thumbs

Gary L. Wilhelm

Magic Thumbs

By Gary Wilhelm

Recently I have witnessed many young people texting on their smartphones. This phenomenon is fascinating. They hold the phone in one or both hands, and use their thumbs to text. The thumb action is incredible. After observing this, I tried it with my smartphone. I ended up dropping the phone on the floor. I then held the phone with one hand and hunted and pecked with my index finger on the other hand.

Well, there must be a way to do this. Maybe it just takes practice. I tried over and over again, but did not achieve any improvement. What is it? Is there some secret? I asked several people I observed doing this, but they all just moved away from me without giving me the secret. Wow, this must be a closely guarded secret. What are they trying to do...limit me to the past century? Maybe I can pay someone to show me how. Is the secret protected by laws? I went downtown and to find someone on a notorious corner downtown, who will tell me for a reasonable price? Nope that didn't work either, but one person did try to sell me something else that might help. No, I don't think that would help.

I decided maybe young people today have different thumbs that allow this...different from the thumbs those of us that were born awhile ago have. I wondered if this change was due to evolution over many years or was this an abrupt change at some point. Darwin did not provide any clue. I tried Google to learn when this change occurred. Did it happen at the turn of the century? Was it in the 1980s? Or was it one of the big changes from the very volatile 1960s. Maybe it was the result of WW 2?

I went to the Orthopedics department at the University Medical School in search of an answer. Do these young people today have different thumbs or what? They told me that thumbs have not changed. They prescribed special, very expensive physical therapy for me. After multiple unsuccessful physical therapy sessions, the U of M suggested there must be something else wrong with me. Perhaps if I would see their even more expensive psychiatrist, that would help me. Unfortunately I had discovered another hole in our health care system. I will report it to AARP for immediate action.

I decided I could not afford their solid gold psychiatrist or his outrageously expensive pills. I am giving up on my thumb dexterity for smartphones. I give a thumbs-up for those with all that dexterity, but personally, I am going back to smoke signals for communicating.

Learning

Carolyn Wilhelm

Learning

By Carolyn Wilhelm

"There was an old woman who lived in a shoe, who had so many children she didn't know what to do!" squawked Mother goose.

"That's funny! But, what's a shoe?" said Downy.

"A shoe? Well, sometime we will probably see a fisherman catching one," explained Mother goose.

"What's a fisherman?" asked Squeak.

"A fisherman? Well, we will probably see one some morning." Mother goose was getting exasperated.

"What is morning?" asked Peep.

"Morning, oh, that's easy. That is when we wake up and

start the day. The sun comes up then." Mother goose felt a little relieved.

"What's the sun?" asked Meep.

"The sun? It's that hot yellow spot in the sun, and don't stare, it can hurt your eyes," answered Mother goose.

"What are eyes?" asked Leap.

"Eyes? My eyes are seeing your parents coming to pick you up! Whew!"

"Bye!"

The next morning, Mother Goose wondered if she had to return to the school.

"Yes, you do," said Father goose. "You are the kindergarten teacher, after all."

Memory

of a Snowflake

Lise Spence-Parsons

Memory of a Snowflake

By Lise Spence-Parsons

She looked out of the window and watched the snow flakes beginning to fall from the darkening sky. Victoria, never Vicky, was all alone in her house. She had been alone for many years.

She thought back to when she and her husband bought the house in 1958. She had been a mere youngster, 25 years old and recently married to Peter. Peter and Victoria, the perfect couple, she a trained nurse, now expectant mother and Peter an architect. They were considered an up-and-coming couple, a golden couple of their generation; to have bought a house in their neighborhood at such a young age was remarkable. She thought of the housewarming party that she and Peter had thrown that spring of 1958. All their friends had attended and the evening had been fantastic with food, wine and dancing to Frank Sinatra with some Elvis music thrown in for good measure. Most of those friends were no longer with them, she'd only just said a final goodbye to Patricia earlier in the week. Victoria smiled to herself, remembering all the antics that she and Patricia had got up to in the early 50's before they settled down to have families. Having a husband and children did change them a lot, but they remained friends and had many fun times. The snow was falling fast now and the fading light was bringing

71

the street lights on. Funny, there weren't as many street lamps when they'd first moved in, as now.

There were only a few houses in the close. Victoria and Peter had known all the people who had moved in and then moved away. They'd lived here from new until now. Well she still lived here, Peter was gone these last six years. He died in 2012 from kidney cancer, a horrible death. She felt a tear roll down her cheek.

The 1960's brought change to the close. People were excited for a new decade, possible space exploration, new music and fashions and some sustainable economy growth was promised to all. Victoria had been excited to try the new fashions and make-up that was available to most women. She learnt to drive and Peter bought her a zippy sports car, bright red. She loved it to bits and took the two children they now had, to play dates, the zoo, or wherever they wanted to go. She'd felt fantastic. She and Peter had lived a perfect life!

The 1960's were years of happiness and then extreme sadness in 1964 when Kennedy was assassinated in Dallas. Victoria remembered watching the news reel on TV, it seemed surreal that he could be murdered in daylight on a drive through a major city in a motorcade. She spooled on in her head and recalled the night of the moon landings in the summer of 1969, the whole world tuning into radio or TV broadcasts, everyone felt connected in that moment of history.

The 1970's were a period of upheaval for Victoria, the anti-war marches, women's rights marches, the Watergate scandal and the births of their third and fourth children all brought conflict and strife to Victoria and Peter. Peter, now had a good middle management job in his architect's firm and they had enough money to extend their house by adding a four-season porch. Victoria kept busy with the two children and found herself pregnant in 1972 with their third. However, they were not to get the third child, Victoria miscarried and the baby was lost to them. It nearly destroyed them, Peter spent hours at the firm and Victoria brooded around the house finding fault with every small thing. Eventually they agreed to counseling and made it to the end of 1975 without further mishap. Victoria thought women had it easy now, she and her generation had fought for women's rights in the 70's, equal pay for the same job, Roe v Wade, she'd been there, marched and waved banners, been arrested and then released. Then in 1976, they got welcome news, Victoria was pregnant again, she vowed to be more careful, she was considered an older mother, in fact ancient, and her doctor told her not to expect too much. But they defied all the odds and David was born to them on a cold but sunny day in March 1977. They were ecstatically happy, their family complete, two girls and now a boy. The snow was now half an inch deep on the ground, and the flakes were getting bigger and faster. She watched as a neighbor's car skid and almost spin out on the road, whilst trying to turn up their own driveway.

The 1980's hit, with all its madness and frenetic money-making schemes. "Fame" was on TV and David loved to watch that, himself dreaming of an acting career. The girls were already in high school and preparing for college within a few years. Peter and Victoria struggled to find things in common. Peter worked all the time or was involved in his golf. She like to meet friends and go the museums, go shopping and visiting the health spa. Victoria noticed that Peter was acting strangely and she suspected an affair. She tried to find out, but it was difficult, he was good at hiding his tracks and could almost make them disappear like footprints in the snow.

It was late, and she'd been up all day sorting memories and items into boxes. She'd continue tomorrow. She fell into an intense dream about her life, all mixed up and confused, a bit like her really.

The next morning it was still snowing, she could hear people shoveling their driveways and the plow came around and cleared the road. It was deep on the sidewalk, there must be at least seven inches of snow, she thought to herself. Her home help, Sally, was there, making her some breakfast,

"Hello Victoria, how was yesterday after I left?"

"Good, I packed a bit and sat by the window watching the snow and remembering my life here."

"I bet, 60 years, is a long time to stay in one place!"

"Not just a place, my home! My husband and three children lived here too, so many memories."

Sally placed the prepared food in front of Victoria. "Are the kids coming today?"

"Yes, I think so, this afternoon to help me with the final pieces of packing and loading."

"Good, then I will see you tomorrow at Serene Willow Park, Victoria. Bye."

"Bye."

She went back to her window seat and started back remembering the 1990's, the girls were both married, had jobs and were planning on having their own children in a few years. They had it all, job, husband and kids, she'd had to make choices, she felt cheated in a way. But then in another way, they only got bits of the pie, she had one whole pie of life. Yes, one whole pie. She smiled. David was in college when he finally realized that acting would probably not pay the bills, so he was working towards a business degree. Then he could pursue acting in his spare time. Good days. Peter had got over his affair, she'd pretended not to have noticed. It fizzled out, maybe the other woman wanted more than he was willing to give, the nagging started and it all was probably more bother than it was worth. He came back to her and the children. They'd never spoken of it openly. She watched the neighbors scraping cars and setting off to work, she wondered if they'd miss her?

Victoria started to giggle at her memories of 1999 New Year's Eve, with everyone fussing if their toaster would work the next day. People anxiously plugging things in and then opening front doors and confirming all was okay. It was not the end of life as we knew it! What a fantastic money making scheme that whole thing had been. She continued to giggle. The new century brought them retirement, David finally retiring in his late 60's, the other partners almost having to push him out, he could not believe he was done, could he trust them to keep the firm going? He eventually settled into a new life style and they began to find common ground again. Victoria saw some children making a snowman in their front yard. They were the fifth family to have lived in that particular house. All had children and they all made snowmen, some things did transcend the decades.

It wasn't until 2006 that Peter felt ill, not really ill and the progression to full blown kidney cancer was not made until 2009, however, it was way too late to treat it successfully. The last few months were agony. He was in terrible pain and in late 2012, he passed away in the hospice with his family at his side, at the age of 80. Victoria remembered that day so clearly, but the days after and since were not so clear and now it was time to pack up the house and leave. The children said it was for the best, to be in a home with full one-on-one care. She could relax and not worry about things. They would be done for her. She looked across the street, at the snowman making children being ushered inside. It was starting to snow again. She looked at her watch, two o'clock already!

The front door opened, Claire, Samantha and David all came in, bundled up from the cold.

"Hello Mum, how are things?"

She hated being asked how 'things' were, "I'm fine," she answered, "just tired."

"The moving van is almost here. The men can load it all and we can get you settled."

"Yes, I know it's time to go, my whole life was here you know. It's not easy to just leave."

The van came, and the men loaded the van. It did not take long to load the last few boxes of Victoria's life. She looked out of the window for the last time, saw darkness falling, people shoveling again, wheeling out waste trash bins for the next day. The day she wouldn't be here any more.

She got into David's red car, which brought back memories of her red zippy sports car in the 50's, and smiled. The snow crunched under the tires as they left.

Dreaming

A Conversation with Myself

Sybil Swanson

Dreaming

By Sybil Swanson

A Conversation with Myself

What do I want to be when I grow up?

But I am grown up, I say.

Yes, but what do I REALLY want to be when I grow up?

I haven't a clue, I say.

Could I be more than I am right now? Could I do more than I do right now?

Sometimes I think, Oh yes, I can be more, I can do more.

Then I think, no, I am what I am. I can't be more. I can't do more.

It's too late, I say.

Oh, I think, how restrictive, how restraining, how depressing. I have forgotten how to dream.

Dream? Dream? I ask.

What does it mean to dream? Isn't living just doing things as life unfolds? Reacting? Surviving?

What's this dream business? I ask.

Dream? Can one really dream when it seems life is almost

gone? Isn't it too late? Isn't it?

Dream? Well, maybe, but what would my dream look like?

I haven't a clue I say.

I've forgotten how to dream.

Well try, I say. Pretend. Remember back to when you dreamed of your life, your future in your teenage years.

Remember? Yes, I can remember lying on my bed gazing out the window, but what did I dream then?

Oh, I remember...silly stuff, silly pipe dreams, pie-in-the-sky stuff, silly romantic stuff. Nothing that could be real someday.

Someday? I ask.

Yes, I remember. I remember saying, Someday I'll be...; Someday I'll do...; Someday I'll live...; Someday I'll have... Someday.

Have I become? Have I done? Have I lived? Has "Someday" happened? I ask.

"Someday" is happening, I reply. This IS "someday".

Well, if "someday" was part of my dream, then maybe I better start dreaming again.

Time is passing. Life is passing. Someday is passing.

Yes, I best get dreaming again!

Written years ago...rediscovered October 2019

Bungee Jumping

With

Sandhill

Cranes

David Zander

Bungee Jumping with Sandhill Cranes

By David Zander

It had been several years since his wife's death from lung cancer and Gavin felt that grief had overstayed its welcome. He had not found out how to get rid of such an uninvited guest. Gavin attended a downtown grief coalition and had taken courses on mindfulness meditation. What more could one do? His loved one had blown away like a fallen leaf in the autumn chill.

He often felt a loneliness especially in the evening at home. The nightly local news was a depressing litany of shootings, deaths, tragedies, floods, forest fires, hurricanes, and tornados. Amazing how many cars were crashing into homes or store fronts, and cars and semis veered across lanes to kill people in head-on crashes. He himself had seen a teenager turn left in front of him going the wrong way onto an exit ramp from the freeway. Even PBS Twin cities public television seemed to be saturated by hours of detectives of all sizes and gender solving murder mysteries - Father Brown, Foyle's War, Inspector Blake, and Vera to name a few and one click away endless histories and documentaries about genocide from Hitler's Germany to Burma (Myanmar) Syria, Turkey and Yemen.

One bright spot was Nova and the nature programs. One night he watched a naturalist talk about the Sandhill crane migration on the Platte River in Nebraska. He decided he should make an effort and go but not alone. He called the local Audubon chapter to see if any groups went from Minnesota. A helpful young woman told him she knew of two guides, Bird Chic and Stan Tekeila. He googled Bird Chic. She made him laugh. She was sitting in a bubble bath with a small camera. Her husband came in. She waved a small camera at him. When the husband left she then brought up to the surface her new huge expensive camera like a submarine surfacing. Gavin called Bird Chic but she was going to Puerto Rica not Nebraska. On Monday Gavin traced Stan Tekeila to the Eden Prairie Parks and Recs. He left a message.

"Are you taking any groups to Nebraska this spring?"

Stan returned his call. "I am leaving Thursday and I have one place left." Gavin called the Park and Recreation and reserved his space. Stan Tekeila was amazing. He did everything. Drove the fourteen seat van, made reservations for hotels and secured space in observation blinds at native centers along the river. Thus it was that a few days later Gavin stood on a back road bridge over the Platt River near Grand Island watching the whole sky as far as the eye could see fill with birds descending on the ninety mile stretch of river. There were over half a million gathering here nightly for safety from predators on the sand bars as they had done for millions of years. Mating dances, conversing before spiraling away to places as far as Alaska and Siberia. It was thrilling to watch. He felt his spirits rise. This was one of the wonders of the world just a day's drive from Minneapolis.

If evenings were dense skyscapes, mornings were like a seat in a darkened theatre before the curtain went up. Gavin had set two alarm clocks and his iPhone, and had got up at 4.30 a.m., a miracle in itself, for he was a night owl and could count the sunrises he had seen on his fingers. Now he was stumbling along rough grassy path silently in single file across a field before sun rise. The group entered the blind by the back door on the side away from the river. Inside he found two rows of wooden bleachers. He sat his eyes adjusting to the gloom in this dark oblong shed near the water's edge. The front was slats you could see through. The sound of cranes was loud. They did not appear to sleep but talked to each other all night long.

Slowly, as the sun rose, the area outside the blind before him transformed from gloomy misty dark greys into a slightly more colored panorama of thousands of throbbing moving shapes, twenty thousand or more cranes some as close as a few yards away from where he was the invisible observer. The bird watchers were in a quiet frenzy of camera world. He sat content to just absorb this scene and use binoculars.

What do you do in such a scene? It is the same problem as on a coral reef teeming with fish. Where to put one's attention. Gavin had taught himself to focus on one small detail. After about half an hour of letting his vision travel from close ups to the far shore and upstream and downstream he began to focus on one stretch of sand bar. He had wondered if the Sandhill cranes would all suddenly take off in a deafening flurry of wings. But that was not what was happening. Small groups would suddenly lift themselves airborne. He could not identify a cue they were responding too. Over the next hour or so the crane population slowly thinned out as groups took to the sky. Other groups zoomed past the window.

Gavin was drawn to one young fledgling who was pointing upstream in a group all facing the other way. It was very attentive to its mother. Gavin became enchanted by this crane. He felt waves of compassion. He felt teary eyed. Death was always a fact of life now. He breathed out mindfully thinking "Please young crane have a safe year and return safely next spring."

How could hunters shoot down these beautiful red capped birds? These hunters included his Brother- in- law who said "ah yes, Sandhill cranes, we call them the ribeye of the sky." As a Buddhist he was supposed to embrace everyone but he loathed these hunters, so different from himself. They seemed to just trap, shoot and kill anything that moved beavers, moose, elk, rabbits, salmon, lion, and Sandhill cranes. He had never fired a gun in his life except a Roy Rogers cap gun as a boy, but now he wanted a license to be able to shoot those obese CEO safari trophy hunters. Put their taxidermy heads up on a trophy wall. The first one would be that Minnesota dentist who had killed old Cecil the lion out

in Uganda. Hang his carcass up to dry on a lamppost outside his dental practice in Bloomington or Cabela's – dentist jerky. Not what you would expect from a Buddhist. Gavin was not a bird watcher or a photographer. When people asked do you have any pictures he tapped his head. "Yes in here." He had pictures stored in his brain from around the world. The closest to this Sandhill crane migration was thousands of miles away on another continent camping on a ledge high over a lake in Kenya looking down on a lake with millions of flamingoes below. And at sunset watching red birds fly into trees in a marshy area of Trinidad's coast.

It was also strange that one other person from East Africa had a presence here. There were write ups in the local nature centers about how Jane Goodall came frequently to the wildlife refuge and worked hard to try to protect the stretch of Platte River as a the sanctuary for of the cranes. Gavin started to feel himself merge with the cranes. And that is when a surprising image surfaced. He had been feeling that grief was like being trapped in a bungee jumping harness high up on a platform over a gorge. At any moment during a day he could be pushed off this platform and hurtle down. He was the reluctant bungee jumper. He saw his wife plunging down smashing in the river on the rocks below. It was like he was following her but then he would be jerked to a halt just feet from the river and oscillate up and down until he became stationary, poised above the river. But now the cranes were flying around him pecking at the bungee cord and harness. They were releasing him. He felt his wings stretching. The young fledging took the last peck that broke the rope and the cranes formed a V shape around him and they glided in formation. It was exhilarating. Then they guided him safely down and showed him how to land on a sand bar.

Gavin woke up in the blind. He had dozed off. The fledgling crane was still out there. It turned as if looking in his direction then turned and faced downstream with the others and the group of about twenty rose and flew up into the air taking his sadness with them. This was a different kind of grief. They were alive and leaving. He softly said "Farewell my friend. Be safe. I will think of you and send thoughts of loving kindness to you for the rest of my life." Gavin settled into a meditation. "Breath in I cherish myself.

Breath out I cherish all sentient beings."

Later he wrote in his journal that the time spent with the cranes marked a significant shift in his grief journey. It was a transition into a life where he would be having new experiences. He still grieved his wife but the lesson learned was that there could be moments of joy. His wife would not want him living in seclusion like some Victorian widow shrouded in black. She would want him out in nature. Some dance with wolves, hug gorillas, feed chimpanzees, breed pandas and Andean frogs, rescue whales, eagles, dolphins. Gavin flies with the cranes. The unwanted bungee jumping down into grief stopped.

He felt he had to grope forward to a new state of mind and go out into the world and begin to live again with feelings of joy and peace. He did not know how much time he had left on this beautiful planet, but he felt that it was healing to be out in nature. And so began the next chapter of his life.

Suggested reading:
Sandhill and Whooping Cranes: Ancient Voices from America's Wetlands by Paul A, Johnsgard.
University of Nebraska Press (2011)
Birds of Minnesota: Field Guide by Stan Tequila (1998)

Fences

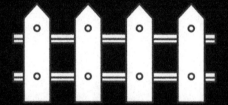

M.M. Jayne

Fences

By M.M. Jayne

Nobody could really pinpoint when it started. The Sheridans and Harleys had been friends since Bob and Tanya Harley moved in next door, nearly 35 years ago. Marilyn Sheridan was the first neighbor to knock at their door, chirpily welcoming them to the neighborhood and offering up homemade strawberry jam. The couples met to play cards at each other's houses once a week. Over the years, their children were born, then running and playing across the lawns, eventually growing up and going off to college and cul-de-sacs of their own. The Friday night card games continued.

Marilyn would later say it all started with that car. After his retirement last fall, Harold Sheridan had taken a full pension and bought a 1959 Ford Galaxie. The car looked like a red Batmobile, with shiny fins, chrome polished to within an inch of its life. It didn't fit in the driveway with his wife's Honda Civic, so he moved Marilyn's car to the patch of grass next to the drive and pulled his car in, dead center on the pavement. He stored it in the garage at night, ignoring Marilyn's bitter asides about old men and stereotypes and how he'd better be out scraping the ice off in the winter before she had to go to work.

In addition to classic cars, Harold had another hobby – a

randy temperament that he'd apparently kept under wraps during his years as an accountant. He began to show up all over town. Ladies wondered out loud at the Women's Auxiliary meeting if he hadn't suffered some sort of neurological event, like a stroke or aneurysm. This brought a guffaw from the back of the room.

Betty Miller crowed. "He was just like that in high school, always pinching butts and winking. You youngsters never knew him except as Mr. Button-up Church Elder, but he was a real actor." She continued cackling to herself. The others turned back around with eye rolls and head shakes. Betty Miller knew everything. All the time.

Bob Harley wondered aloud over breakfast about the property line when he saw that the Sheridans' Civic left bare grass and wheel ruts. He carefully seeded and fertilized his lawn in the spring and fall, ceremoniously setting up sprinklers. His lawn was a lush green that looked like it would be wonderful to picnic on, but no one ever did. Harold's lawn was serviceable, but it didn't take much time for the car to flatten and kill the grass. It bothered Bob more each day, but he still smiled and waved at Harold and played cards with him every Friday night.

The problem of the grass really started to feed on Bob's mind, especially after Tanya told him about the knee rubs under the table and butt pat that had started happening whenever she went to the kitchen on card nights. Harold would offer to help out, coming in close behind her, chuckling at his own jokes. She would return to the card table, furiously blushing, making some joke about hot flashes. Her ears burned.

"Oh, he's just joshing you, honey." With just the briefest pause, Bob said, "I'm thinking about putting up a fence. It's really getting on my nerves - that patch of ruts on one side."

Tanya fiddled with her collar. She felt anxious, her mind precariously balancing thoughts like a Jenga game, block teetering on block, each moment a little less steady than the last.

"I'm fed up with it and with..." She sighed and stomped her way out of the room. Her husband was already making notes about the dimensions of the fence.

Marilyn and Bob came over Friday night. Tanya laid out cheese and crackers and sliced deli meat, a plate of cookies, and had made sure the fridge was stocked with wine for the ladies and beer for the men. She smoothed the table runner mindlessly while checking her makeup in the mirror. They arrived promptly. Bob as boisterous and rosy-cheeked as ever, Marilyn smiling primly, holding out a plate of brownies. Tanya took the plate from her with a muttered thanks and headed directly to the kitchen.

"So, Tanya dear, how's your quilt coming along?" Tanya appeared not to hear Marilyn's question. She regretted telling Marilyn about the class she took at Sew Finery, with a mumbling teenager and wizened man named Larry who spit on the material in front of him whenever he talked. Every time Marilyn saw Tanya, she asked her about progress on the quilt. Tanya simmered. The quilt was stuffed in an upstairs closet, mangled and unfinished, loose threads trying to make an escape.

She always said, "Almost done."

Marilyn didn't understand her recalcitrance, but then she always thought Tanya was a porcupine - prickly and defensive. Marilyn often thought about what animals people were. It seemed easier to put up with them. Harold had gone from a wolf to a wild boar over the course of their marriage. She'd leave him except that there was really nowhere to go.

She was a tortoise. Whatever fantastical journeys she'd

imagined taking as a girl had long since disappeared, swallowed whole by the voracious needs of others. She'd held the line up until her 40s and then it became too tiring to pretend that she could be anything more than "helpful Marilyn." She kept working at the library, sunk into her body, kept her hands busy and a smile at the ready.

Tanya rose to refill her wine glass.

"She doesn't need any help in the kitchen, Harold." Bob's voice cut across the room, just as Harold began to rise out of his chair. Bob's tone was flat and he didn't look at Harold as he dealt the next round. When Tanya came out of the kitchen, she could barely contain her smile. And it wasn't directed towards Harold. Marilyn looked back and forth between the two men. For the rest of the night, she said very little and when Harold put his arm around her to wish the Harleys a good night, she wanted to cry.

It wasn't until the following Tuesday morning that Harold knew something was happening. He watched through the kitchen window as Bob gestured to two men. He recognized Tim Markham from the city surveyor's office. The other man wore a jean shirt with a name tag and was pointing to the strip of lawn between the houses. Normally, he'd wander out, coffee in hand and find out what was going on, but since last Friday, he avoided Bob.

The fence work started three days later, after orange paint marked the property line and red marked another foot back where city ordinance would allow a fence to be. The work was started shortly after Marilyn had left for work. Harold had gone to a car show in Rockport. His car wasn't an entrant, but he liked to hang out in the parking lot where classic cars were chatted over and admired. When Harold returned, Marilyn's car was in the driveway. He'd worked up a good head of steam by the time he walked through the front door.

"Give me your keys. I don't know why we have to play these games. I told you I'd be back by 6."

Without looking up from her book at the kitchen table, she extended her arm, keys dangling passively from her fingers. He snatched them away and stormed back outside.

That's when he noticed the pile of lumber and the van in the drive next door. Northco Fencing. *So that was that*, he thought. He moved Marilyn's car to the street and pulled the Galaxie into the garage. He had to move her car back on the drive or else the mailboxes would be blocked and Ed, the postal carrier refused to deliver the mail when there were cars in front of the boxes.

He sat in his wife's car, feeling the anxiety rising up past his pounding heart. Beads of sweat pearled on his forehead. It had been a faux retirement. The partners had given him no choice. It seemed like he'd become a ghost, haunting his home, drifting the streets where real people had jobs and women noticed men. He remembered the woman's face when he'd smiled and winked at her at the coffee shop. Just a hint of disgust before she pasted on a smile. He didn't know how to live in this world.

Marilyn glanced up and was alarmed to see her husband standing in the doorway. He was very pale.

"Don't you feel well?" She prepared to leap into action, grab a thermometer, an ice pack, an ibuprofen.

Harold shook his head and sank down into the chair across from her. They sat in silence, the pounding of nails punctuating the seconds.

Minnesota

Gardens

Caroline Munro

Minnesota Gardens

By Caroline Munro

Autumn displays her flamboyant colors for a dizzying few weeks of faded tapestry tones. They blaze like flames across my garden landscape of maples, velvet sumac and silver birch. Every leafy bough rejoices in colors of burning jade, amber, garnet and ruby. The amethyst leaves of Venetian Sumac, have frost dipped edges. They flex their frozen veins, snap with a sigh and drop to the glittering grass.

A pheasant in its glossy plumage struts carefully onto the frozen creek. It tilts its head and pecks at the ice, peering deeply into the water beneath the thin crust. Its small head mechanically darts to and fro, stabbing at dark fish that can still be seen through the precarious veil of ice. The fish dart for cover in deeper water, seeking the murky vegetation and mud for winter hibernation, there they will wait for Spring's first kiss to wake them from their icy dreams.

Tall grasses line the edges of the creek, their dried fronds frozen in the last sway of summer's breeze, crystalized by the sparkling breath of approaching winter. Felled trees lie like slumbering giants on the shoreline, a light dusting of hoarfrost shimmers on their gnarled wood and tortured limbs. Long taloned fingers stretch out into the rotting leaves and mud. The tangled roots wrenched from the creek's bank, claw for a foothold but lie defeated, arms outstretched in submission to the sky.

A ferret scurries across the creek, weaving its lithe body through the jungle of grasses. It ducks under dead wood, sniffing the frigid air, carefully looking for predators, or prey, with its sharp beady eyes. Small feet pad noiselessly over the damp carpet of decaying leaves, twigs and autumn debris. Suddenly its gone, a last glimpse of tail as it disappears into its lair.

A flash of azure blue streaks across the morning sky, as two bluejays greedily swoop on the fallen acorns of my lawn. Noisily they call a warning to each other and leap in perfect unison to the tall limbs of a nearby pine tree. They cackle angrily at a fat squirrel that has disturbed their banquet. Busily he buries his plunder in the crisp earth, memorizing each cache of food for the deprivation of winter. His tail twitches a warning as he sits back on his plump haunches, filling his distorted cheeks with food. Miniature hands work busily, pushing acorns into his mouth, working the food round and round as his sharp teeth relentlessly bite into the hard shell of the nut.

The morning sun rises higher in the sky and heads East, stretching its rose tinted rays over the garden, softly melting the transient frost and arousing the slumbering autumn dawn into a beautiful Indian summer day, The warmth of the sun stirs up the musty stench of fallen leaves, this earthy smell conjures up the exotic wares of an Indian market, where heaps of spices draw you in with their mystical aroma. Cinnamon, ginger, saffron and turmeric. The colors of autumn foliage imitate the natural dyes of a hand woven rug, tooled leather and baskets of the exotic East, nature and craft united by the senses. Stretches of rich color on the trees and bushes take you on a magic carpet ride of the imagination, to the sultan's palace of luxurious velvets, patterned damask and heady spices.

Piled leaves, wind swept against bushes and grasses, tumbled onto the fragile glass of the creek, caught in the limbs of trees or pressed wet against the dark soil, offer up their musky scent to the heavens, a decaying tribute to the Gods of summer.

December

Day

Marj Helmer

December Day

By Marj Helmer

Whirling. Swirling.

Small, medium, huge.

One, six, ten and more.

Through the day,

Into the night.

Fireplace glowing.

Beautiful from the inside.

Surging to go out.

Piling layers, pulling boots,

Mittens, scarves.

Then out the door.

Face first to revel deep within.

On the back, legs and arms sweeping.

Tongue outthrust to taste.

Pulling into the garage.

Snow cascading off the car.

Smashing and towed cars behind.

Solid floor and quiet wipers.

Inside. The roast is in the pot.

Catch Me
If You Can

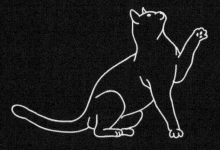

Sybil Swanson

Catch Me If You Can

By Sybil Swanson

I love a lot of things. I've even made a list for you of a few of my favorite things. These aren't necessarily in the order of my preferences, but those preferences change from day to day anyway.

I love to dominate...ALL the time.

I love to plop down in the middle of the floor. Just to lay there. I like it even better if it's in the middle of the kitchen floor and you are trying to fix dinner.

Other things I love to do? I love to play when it's time for bed and you are sooooooooo tired.

Love it, when I can rub against you and leave my scent. The bonus is, I can also leave some of my fur on you. It works on furniture too.

Love it when you pet me, until I don't. Love to bite too.

Love it when you dangle a toy on a string that I can try and capture, until I don't. I easily get bored with such things.

Love it when there is an open window and I squish between the blind slats to peer out the window and all you see is my butt, but the neighbors see my pretty side. Love it that now the slats are bent and it's easier to get through the next time.

Love it when I cough up a fur ball. They can be so irritating. Then you scrub and scrub until that horrible thing is all gone. Thank you.

Love it, when I play catch-me-if-you-can. Best game ever! That's when you try to catch me to get me off your bed when you are trying to make the bed. It's especially fun when you are changing the sheets. I can spin and leap; yep, leap straight up in the air and you miss catching me every time. Crawling under the fitted sheet is even more fun, and then the top sheet is even better to crawl under. That's such fun. I crawl under the sheet and stay there as you try to edge me off, but I scoot to a different spot and play the game again and again. Fun, fun, fun. Finally, you get a hold of me and suddenly, I am airborne...not by choice. Hate that.

Love it when you open the outside door and I play, "Freedom!" and I scoot out the door. Problem with that is I sniff and sniff at all the delicious smells. I just can't help it. That's when you catch me. Not so fun.

Love it, when you lay down on the sofa and I leap up onto your tummy and then circle once or twice, lay down and fall asleep. Excuse me, fall BACK to sleep. You are always so puzzled how I know you have laid down since I was in another part of the house fast asleep.

You always accuse me of sleeping with one eye open. You are right. I do just that! This is a talent I have, just to make you marvel at how wonderful I am.

I have so many talents that I can even squeeze through incredibly slim spaces or curl up in the smallest of spaces. I can hop in and out of any box. Oh, I do love boxes. I can play "hide-n-seek" in a box. I believe you can't see me, but I can see you. Such fun. You think I'm crazy. I'm just letting off steam. Try it. Really healthy for you.

I love, love, love to chase things. Even those teeny tiny things you can't seem to see. Drives you crazy, especially when I use you as my springboard to get up high to where they are flying.

I am the greatest at staring you down, but it gets even better when I just sit and look at you. Then you invariably, ask "What?". Then you repeat yourself when I continue to just look at you. You again ask, "What, what do you want?" You get so nervous, as if I know something you don't, and you think I can tell you. That is soooooooooooo funny.

That's something else you do; you talk to me as if you were going to get an answer. Love it.

Just a reminder: I am not a human, so I can't understand your language, much less speak it. You make it far too difficult to communicate. My kind keep it simple. We can communicate just fine using only one word: MeeeOOOOw.

Life

By Candle

Light

Sarah Bromage

Life By Candlelight

By Sarah Bromage

This is the story of a pair of silver candlesticks that are three hundred years old. These candlesticks belonged to my great grandparents on my mother's side and probably before that. They all were very wealthy Victorian and late Georgians. As a child I used to love seeing these candlesticks on the dining table in Camden, Sidmouth. They shimmered against the polished mahogany table. I could never understand why they were never used. They appeared to have a very gracious existence. The family crest is too hard for me to identify but the dates were 1711 and 1713. It was the end of the reign of Queen Ann and the beginning of the reign of George 1st. I often wonder who the first people were to use these candlesticks. Imagine the draughty houses, amazing costumes and life that were as different then as from today. Even in the time I know my family owned them there was no electricity and life was elegant but not that we would be familiar with. Granny tried to sell them in the early 60s after my grandfather died but as they were not a pair in date they were not then saleable. She was offered three thousand pounds I believe but declined. Three thousand pounds then would have bought us a nice house in the outskirts of London, or a lovely large old home in Devon. When Camden was split up the candlesticks became my mother's and resided on the same dining table that had been used in Camden. She lived on the Isle of Mull in Scotland. However, she didn't use them either. They have a problem in that there is no lip for the wax to collect in so the wax pours down the candlesticks and often onto the table. Since I inherited them they have been really put to work. They were often in use for dinner parties at Paddocks Cottage in Devon and in use every night here when the winter sets in. I love the gentle light they give off and get through a lot of candles. That's where rummage sales help out greatly. I think they aid the flow of conversation with of course wine as well. Also their light is so much more peaceful than a sharp overhead light.

Due to our plumbing system and common sense when I clean them in boiling water I don't pour the boiling waxy water down the drain. It goes outside to confuse the insects and decorate the river rock. It is frustrating not knowing about their first hundred years or so, but well kept they certainly were. I can only feel for the poor under maids having to clean these beauties along with everything else. Red hands, chipped nails and chilblains.

I gather Marie Antoinette swore by candle light as it doesn't show up blemishes on the face so much. Smallpox was rife at the time which created tremendous scarring. In the meantime I am enjoying my beautiful old elegant pair with their mystery and the fun that I am sure they are having now with us. I really hope one of the family or grandchildren will show an affection and interest in them. They deserve to be used and enjoyed. They have a wonderful atmosphere about them.

Whoever has them next, I hope they are enjoyed and please carry on their history. They are museum pieces but are there to be cherished.

Solar Energy

in Northern

Minnesota

Gary L. Wilhelm

Solar Energy in Northern Minnesota

By Gary Wilhelm

We built a cabin a few years ago in northern Minnesota. We oriented it with the large windows and patio doors facing the south, and a few degrees to the east, hoping we would have some benefit from passive solar to help with heating in the winter. We knew that sky there is overcast or mostly cloudy 63% of the time and mostly clear or partly cloudy 37% of the time. So we really were not counting on a lot of help from solar energy. We knew that in Arizona, southern California, and other states much further south, many people used solar panels to provide some or all of their electricity. We did not expect to see many or any solar panel installations in our neighborhood near the Canadian border. However we soon learned there were more than 100 solar panel installations within a few miles of our cabin. Over the past several years I have been able to visit five or six solar-powered homes.

My first introduction to active solar energy came when we visited some people who have a place-in-the woods, about 10 miles from our cabin near Grand Marais. Their land borders on a gravel road where they keep their car, but to get to their year-round two room home, it is necessary to walk more than 2/3 mile on a narrow path through the woods. The path is on low ground and small streams of water ran across it. Birds are abundant on both sides of the path and the forest seems alive. There are two solar panels on the roof of their cabin, and these two panels provided all of their electricity. A few automobile batteries store electricity for use when there is no sun. They are able to power a miniature refrigerator, several small lights, and are also able to recharge the battery in their laptop computer. The electrical power these two people use is minimal, but it all comes from the sun. They have a shallow well near their house which is pumped by hand. There is an outhouse. All of their heat comes from a small woodstove near the center of their cabin. There is no back-up heat or electricity. They live almost "off-the-grid," but not quite...they have a telephone landline with dial-up internet capability.

During the years after this first visit to a solar-powered cabin, I had an opportunity to visit other people's solar-powered homes. What I saw was quite a wide range of how various people live with a variety of solar energy installations. Some places have many solar panels...sometimes mounted atop a large steel pipe anchored in concrete, sometimes on a standalone aluminum frame built to support them, and/or on the roof of a cabin or garage. Solar provides some or all electricity for each residence. There is a wide range of comfort. Most (but not all) places have running water pumped by electricity, and indoor plumbing with septic systems. Some have their own storage batteries, while other people connect to the electric grid (thereby removing their need for batteries) and sell power back to the power company when they have extra, and buy power when there is no sun. The people who have their own batteries and are not connected to the power grid, seem very pleased when they have electricity, while others do not because the power lines are down. However batteries do require some maintenance. All people did most of their heating with wood, which is quite plentiful in northern Minnesota...either with the furnace separate and outside the home to heat water which was piped into the home to provide heat; or alternatively with small woodstoves inside the home.

One site I visited was a small cabin right on the shore of Lake Superior...again with only two small solar panels, several lights, a small refrigerator, and a small wood stove used for cabin heat, cooking, heating water, etc. There was an outhouse (none of which is pumped out periodically.). But there was no well. All water (drinking and otherwise) was carried from Lake Superior in buckets. Apparently the water is so cold, it is safe to drink. An older retired couple live there. They spend at least one week a month at that cabin...12 months of the year. They also have a small apartment in Minneapolis.

My impression was that the two things which are a problem because of the limitations of solar energy are: heating and cooling. In the woods, many people heat primarily with wood anyway. Air conditioning is not required there because it is quite cool. Even a refrigerator or freezer can be a problem though. Some people had super-efficient refrigerators, Eco-fridge from Denmark...very expensive, but they take less electricity than one 60 watt incandescent bulb. One person also told me about a super-efficient freezer...also from Scandinavia and very expensive.

There is an interesting variety of solar systems. Some people have no backup; others have LP gas backup for heating and also to power a backup electrical generator. The cost of solar panels has come down dramatically in the past few years, and a surprising number of people in the north woods are adding solar panels to their homes and cabins. In the forest near Grand Marais, there are more than 100 systems. Some were chosen because there were no power lines nearby, others for various reasons, including people who are very independent, and some people who want to be "inexpensive" for nature to support, or to have a lower carbon footprint.

I learned that "going solar" has far-reaching ramifications including selection of appliances, and how people actually live. Adding solar to existing buildings looks like it can be especially complicated.

Dance

Class

Caroline Munro

Dance Class

By Caroline Munro

It was 4.45 p.m. The parking lot was full and children were running to and from dance class. This was my family's first encounter with a professionally run dance studio and I had been delaying signing my children up for a year. Well meaning friends had given me dire warnings about the down side of the dance studio. Overbearing mothers, prima donna children, not to mention the cost of tuition and costumes. But my children were insistent that this was what they wanted to do. The sports field held no enticements for them, they wanted to dance and there were no other studios that offered a more casual atmosphere for us to consider. So here we were pushing through the studio's double doors, surrounded by excited children and experienced mothers. Into the lion's mouth we plunged.

The vestibule was plastered with photographs of students from last year's recitals. Children with practiced smiles, standing in suggestive poses with china doll make-up. Neon colored, sparkly jazz outfits, frou-frou tutus with crystal tiaras and skin tight spandex, clamored for ones attention. This was a world so different from our own experience. Here heavy make-up was encouraged, sexy moves were to be mastered and innocent girls were dressed to catch the judge's eyes with jailbait outfits.

I was both fascinated and repelled by these photographs, flashes of Jon Benet Ramsey passed through my mind, as I looked at a picture of five year old girls, wearing platinum wigs, cowboy boots and fringed skirts. I tried to shake off this image, as I saw my daughter's face, full of pure rapture, pointing out the "Barbie doll" pink costume she most wanted. She only saw the excitement of wearing dress-up clothes and imitating her idol Brittney Spears. But I was already feeling myself being sucked into the spiraling costs of costumes, dance shoes, lessons and competition expenses. I had agonized over the new challenges my children were going to have to face in competition. Would it be too much pressure for my happy go lucky kids, to be judged not only on their performance but on their appearance as well? Were we ready to commit to the schedule of rehearsals, weekend competitions and seven days of recital?

Pulling my children to my side, I approached the desk, where three mothers commandeered the phones, fitted and sold dance shoes, coordinated lesson fees and generally tried to control the chaos of children and parents that milled around in the small waiting room. I felt I was being given the "once over" as they spied fresh revenue. "Can we help you?" A large lady with an oversized sweatshirt inquired. This was it, there was no going back. "Yes, I'm interested in starting my son and daughter in dance class. Are there any openings for this winter's schedule?" I felt irrationally nervous, was I expecting them to laugh at my proposal of starting my inexperienced children in this new world of poise and grace? I noticed them weighing up the unexplored talent of my son and daughter. How much competition would they be for these mother's beloved offspring? "Ummmm! You're rather late for this intake, but I think we can squeeze you in to the costume fittings for the Spring recitals. How old is your daughter, about ten?" I nodded in agreement. "Right, well we could fit her into the Monday evening Ballet/Jazz/Tap program. How does that sound?" My daughter Lauren looked up at me, smiling from ear to ear. " Now how about your son? We run a boys "Cool" class which is free to parents who already have another child in the school." Alex was already hopping up and down with excitement. They had him at "Cool".

There was no going back now, we were signed up and all we had to do was purchase shoes and get them both measured up for recital costumes. After paying forty dollars for the class, almost one hundred dollars for the shoes and making the first installment on the costumes, my wallet felt sadly depleted, but it was worth it to see my children's smiling faces. We stepped away from the front desk and decided to have a look at the dancers in each of the three studios.

The hallway was packed with parents, patiently waiting for their offspring. Milling around talking, or sitting on uncomfortable looking benches placed in front of large plate glass windows. Studio one had a pre-school class in progress. This class drew the largest crowd, as anxious mothers gathered at the window. Their children danced to Shirley Temple's "Animal crackers in my soup" which blared loudly over the P.A system. The young dancers tried to master the simple steps. Awkwardly they pointed their toes and wobbled on one leg. Little bellies popped out of ill fitting leotards and "Disney print" knickers hung below their skirts. Laboriously the moves proceeded, with gentle coaxing from the teacher, who whispered their commands and used her fingers to demonstrate each step. The pr-schoolers watched her intently, faces screwed up in concentration, eyes darting to their mothers for encouragement outside. The class ended and each child proudly received a sticker for good work, then trailed out to their proud parents.

We moved over to the window of studio two, which reverberated loudly to the sound of thirty students tap shoes hammering out " I've got rhythm" on the pine wood floor. Feet and hands moved with military precision to the relentless beat, like a machine gun firing silver bullets of sound. Serious faces, cheeks shaking with the impact of steel taps on wood. They had a look of deep concentration on their brows, as they watched their own reflection in the wall to wall mirrors. The teacher shouted out encouragement and direction from the corner of the room, critically studying every mistake in timing and accuracy. Finally the music ended and the students, clutching their sides with stitch or shaking out a tight muscle, relaxed in small clusters to joke and chat. As the studio door opened and they started to exit, the steamy air reached us, hot with their exertion and smelling of warm animal bodies.

Studio three was still in class. High school girls in their ballet lesson started to stretch and warm up. They looked so graceful as they bent and reached out. Willowy arms, long necks and toned bodies extended and relaxed. Years of training made the ballet movements look effortless. Muscled legs and arms, honed in this difficult discipline, made every gesture a photographic feast for the eyes. They stood like graceful statues, heads held high, fingers fanned out in a perfection of detail. These young swans echoed every nuance of the classical piano playing as accompaniment. They were, in my mind, fulfilling the pinnacle of dancing prowess. The music faded and the master class came to its inevitable close. The students politely applauded each other and the teacher, then collected at the door. Young swans returned once more to their high school demeanor, toting heavy back packs, chewing gum, sporting sneakers and baggy jeans.

We were enthralled by everything we had seen. I didn't know if my children had the talent to reach the level of expertise and grace we had just enjoyed, but I knew that they would have fun taking part. After all it's better to have tried and failed then never to have tried at all.

The
Fight

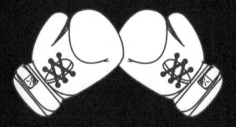

Marj Helmer

The Fight

By Marj Helmer

I looked out my window and saw the three of them in the snow. I liked to watch them play. This time was no different. Two of them fought. The other watched. I wondered which was worse, fighting or watching. They wrestled and rolled around. Who would be the stronger? King of the hill.

The two fighters gave up and chased away. I knocked on the window until the other looked at me. His challenge was clear. I knocked again. Stronger this time. Finally he turned away and bolted after the others. Damned squirrels.

Always
Hope

Sybil Swanson

Always Hope

By Sybil Swanson

I hate this feeling. I feel so lost. Everything is meaningless. Why go on? First Jordan is gone, who was so incredibly special, then Dorie, a dear friend, then Martha my sweetest daughter and now James. All the people who meant so much to me have left me. Is that my problem? Do I feel rejected with them gone, or do I just not know how to identify myself without them a part of me in the here and now? Somehow, I have to get beyond this. I have to find me again. But how do I do that? These people are the ones who made my life have meaning.

Now there's Sara who wants to go out every time we chat. There's John who wants to "get together", whatever that means. Then there's Sandy who wants to go to Thailand and will pay for my expenses. A great offer, but again. I feel no need, no desire, no interest. I've rejected them all. They aren't the answer.

Why isn't there some sort of medication for all these jumbled up feelings? I suppose if I took enough happy pills, I'd feel differently, but that's not the feeling I'm looking for. I want something that would help me make sense of things again, to have some meaning, some depth to life, to living fully again. What do I know that can help get me through this?

That's it! I do know exactly how to get my life back. I have knowledge of the successful 12-step programs. I have the knowledge and the experience of past events all within me. I have been in the darkness of life before and gotten out of it. Yes! I do. I do have the greatest knowledge within me...I have God and my Savior, Jesus. Prayer brings me the peace, the hope, the joy I have lost and must find again. And, I will find it again. There is hope, always hope.

Thank you, God, for life. My life, which You have given me. Thank you, God. You are the answer. Thank you for hearing me, helping me to find the answers, for giving me Your mercy and grace. Amen.

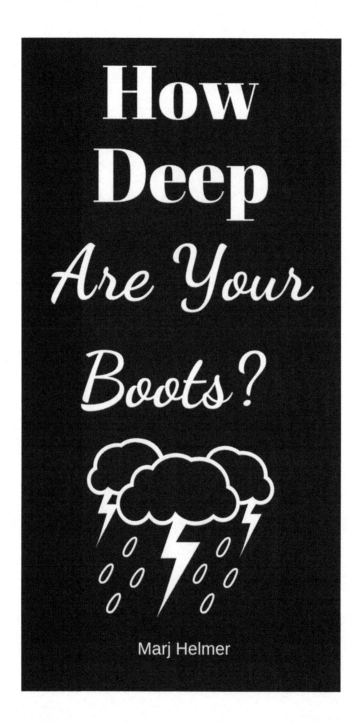

How Deep

Are Your

Boots?

Marj Helmer

How Deep Are Your Boots

By Marj Helmer

Most people do not greet each other in the morning with "How's the weather?" But in those realms where the weather can mean life or death, that is the routine. A little over dramatic? Most places are so civilized that it would be rare to die because of the weather. But it is true, weather can kill.

So, how do we cope? On the east coast, umbrellas are all over. Even on sunny days. On rainy days they're sold on every corner. Shops have stands to hold the soggy ones and for leaving behind or having them stolen, uh, borrowed.

Umbrellas are in Chicago too, but the wind carries them off or blows the rain under. However, the rain isn't going to kill you unless you fall into a pothole and drown.

Out west the rain draining down the streets can sweep you away into the desert to be found maybe days later. Flash floods from far away roll you along in passing and deposit you in odd places and you don't even know they're coming.

Deserts bring up the problems of sun and heat. Severe ultraviolet radiation, aka sunburn, can cause first and second degree burns, DNA destruction, melanoma (cancer), heat stroke and those annoying wrinkles. In humid climbs, dehydration from sweating or not drinking plus the heat can put you in the hospital or kill you.

Then there are tornadoes. Unlike Dorothy, we can be warned if we're listening, but too many have to go out and see or even film the charging, spinning monster. Blizzards can also be foreseen, but too many see them as a challenge. Emergency packs, shovels, blankets, candy bars are packed into cars in November and left until there until May, just in case.

Hurricanes on the east coast are to be "ridden out." After all, the last evacuation wasn't needed. We sat in traffic all day and it only sprinkled.

Winds can tip over boats, blow you over a cliff, topple buildings or sandblast your car. They're part of blizzards and hurricanes too, see above. But we love them. In mild or fierce mode, we see them as romantic, hair blowing, gowns billowing, sweeping moors, ah love.

And don't run under a tree to escape lightening. Or keep playing golf or fishing under grey skies. And it doesn't have to rain to have Ben run his experiment on you.

Weather is a challenge unless you live in San Diego. Otherwise, the answer to the question "How's the weather?" is "How deep are your boots?"

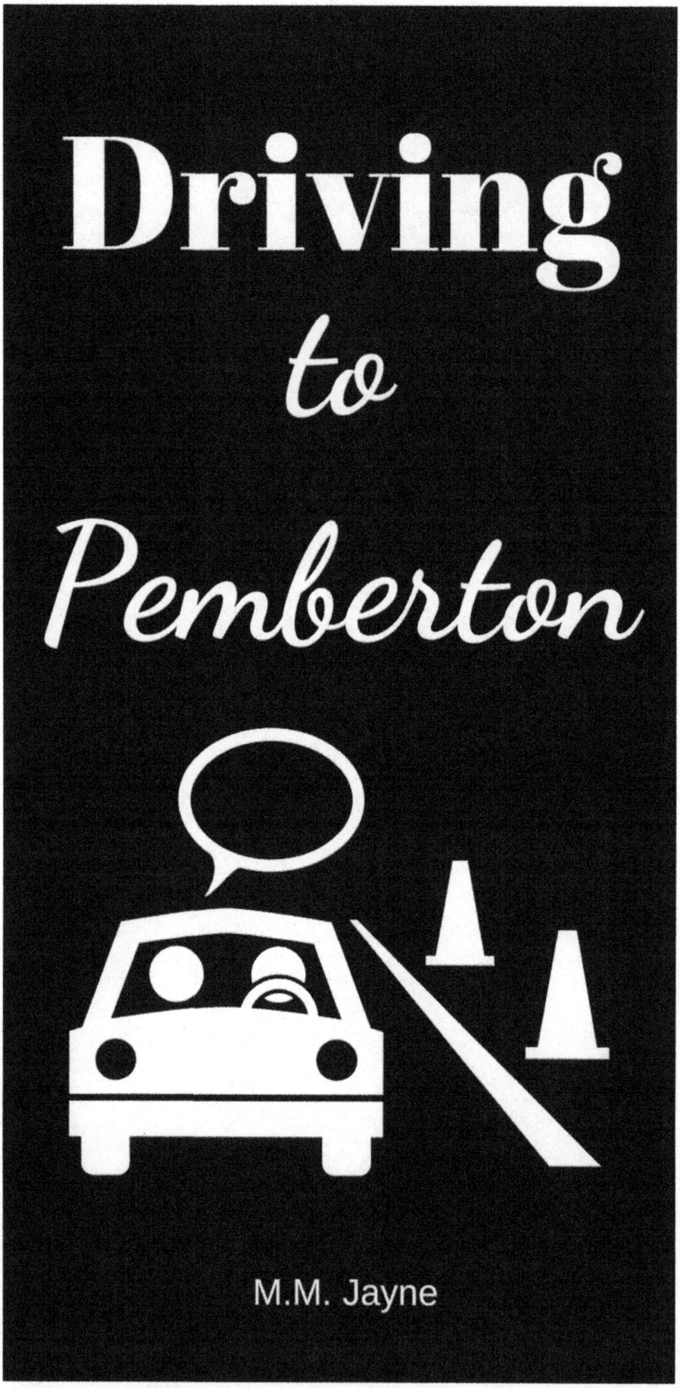
Driving
to
Pemberton
M.M. Jayne

Driving to Pemberton

By M.M. Jayne

The highway meandered through the farmland in front of them, the land flat and graceless with a gloomy sky overhead. Maureen stared morosely out the window. For the last five years, she and David made this drive to her cousin's up in Pemberton to celebrate Christmas - three hours of driving and a stay at a decrepit motor inn. David had already begun his quiet manic humming.

Beth was staying at college this holiday to go on a ski trip with her roommates. Her mother tried to stay lighthearted and wished her a safe trip at the end of their call, but Beth could tell she was near tears. She loved her parents, but a trip to Pemberton could never stand up to laughing around a roaring fire with her chums. "Tell everyone hi, Mom."

Maureen could already hear the muttered "Oh, that's a shame." from several quarters, before her Aunt Gloria piped up with "Does she have a boyfriend?" Or her cousin's husband Bert began making jokes about Beth's field of study. Inevitably it would end up in a heated debate over politics.

"Can we stop at the next rest area?" Maureen fidgeted. David no longer complained about all the stops. A prostate cancer diagnosis a year ago made his own needs more frequent.

The convenience store and gas station looked like the same muddied up version they'd see for the next couple of hours. After a gymnastic feat of using the restroom while touching as few surfaces as possible, Maureen wandered through the aisles.

She turned the corner and nearly ran into a young couple. They were holding hands. They smiled at her apologies and as she passed by, the man muttered something and the woman laughed.

The clerk barely acknowledged her as she paid for a bottle of water and a granola bar. David was at the car, pumping gas. She paused a moment, watching him as he stared off into the neighboring field. He looked so tired these days. Neither of them had been sleeping well.

There was a sense of foreboding that hung on since he went through treatment. The doctors declared it a success with the usual caveats about possible recurrence. It was the possibilities that weighed on him.

"Get what you needed?" He pulled the gas nozzle out of the tank, tapped it and hung it back on the pump. She handed him the granola bar.

They were back on the road. They'd be on time for dinner. The silence felt oppressive to Maureen. David started humming again.

"Do you remember when we first got married and we didn't go anywhere for the holidays?" She tried to speak in a lighthearted tone, but it came across as insistent.

"Yeah, we were too far away from everyone and too broke to travel. What makes you think of that?"

"Remember we used to give each other socks or goofy poems?"

136

"I remember spending at least one Christmas in **only** socks." He smiled and tried to waggle his eyebrows at her.

She started to cry.

"What?" Worry came out sounding like anger.

"I hate this, this waiting..." She began to sob in earnest.

He let out a tight breath and pulled the car onto the highway shoulder and turned off the ignition.

She wiped her nose, but wouldn't raise her eyes to meet his.

"Mo, what's going on?"

"I'm just tired. I'm so tired of worrying about the next doctor visit. I'm so tired of being stuck."

"Well, it isn't my goddamn fault that I got cancer!"

"I'm not blaming you, but we're not happy." Her tone dared him to disagree.

He slumped back in his seat. "Are you leaving me?" He knew it was inevitable, since that day at the Nelsons' party. Maureen looked so small and miserable sitting in a lawn chair. It was a few days after his diagnosis.

She said nothing for a few minutes. Her rage was palpable when she spoke next. "What the hell are you talking about? Why would I leave you?"

David gripped the steering wheel. "You're not happy in our marriage."

"No, I'm not happy with our life. But it's **our** life, right?"

"What does that mean? I don't know what you want."

She opened her purse and handed him a small, wrapped present.

He looked up from a pair of socks, covered in pictures of

goofy-faced reindeer. Puzzled, but a little goofy-faced himself, he leaned over and kissed her.

"What about the presents?"

"We'll mail them."

"The reservation?"

"We'll cancel it."

"Your family?"

She smiled wickedly, "Screw 'em." They burst out laughing.

He started the car, did a U-turn and they headed home.

Be a

Procrastinator

Sybil Swanson

Be a Procrastinator

By Sybil Swanson

I am a procrastinator! Been told a million times that it's not a good idea, it's unhealthy, etc., but I think procrastinators are exciting people, full of vitality.

What is a procrastinator? According to Webster, procrastination is the act or habit of procrastinating, or putting off or delaying, especially something requiring immediate attention. Hey, it says delaying or putting off something, it doesn't say the task is never done.

So it doesn't mean you're not going to do the task, but rather just delay doing the task. Big difference in my book.

What's great about procrastinating is that sometimes it works to your advantage. For instance, in the fall when the leaves are falling from the trees and your lawn is covered, you really don't want to rake them up right now because a really good movie is on TV, or you are in the middle of reading a really good book, so you procrastinate raking those leaves today. You'll do it tomorrow. Lo and behold, tomorrow comes and you find that in the night the wind picked up and blew those leaves right out of the yard and on down the block. Yep, procrastination paid off. Saved you time and energy!

Normally one still must do their projects no matter what, but why not procrastinate and do them when YOU want to do them. Why miss out on those "last-chance-today" offerings. The project will wait for you. I've found they always do.

Another plus for procrastinating: house cleaning. Yes, I could plug along and clean the house for the party this weekend, taking one room a day and get the job done, being very organized and methodical. Of course, this would mean a very boring day, every day. Or, I could procrastinate and enjoy each day until Friday. Wow, Friday already and tomorrow the guests will come. Well, of course the job must get done...NOW! I jump into action, the paintings and furniture get dusted, the carpet gets vacuumed, the clothes get hung up, the newspapers get tossed, the bathroom gets scrubbed and the beds and dishes, well, they'll get done in the morning. So, what has happened? The major differences are: I enjoyed myself for five days; did what I wanted to do; I wasn't bored those five days, plugging along but rather excited and energized getting the job done. The end result was the same. I moved quickly, accomplishing much in a relatively short period of time and became exhausted to the point of collapsing in bed and having a wonderful night's rest.

Of course, when it's job related that's a different story. Not a good idea to procrastinate. Nor when your children or grandchildren need you, or when the house is on fire. Those are times when you must be quick in taking action or making a decision, getting the job done...NOW. No procrastination allowed. Procrastinators can make quick decisions. They've trained themselves to do so when time has run out. This is excellent training.

I believe procrastinators have a sixth sense and know what can and can't be put off. Our leaders must make quick decisions, getting the job done. They too are probably procrastinators. Mom and Dad, your procrastinating child may be one of our future leaders.

Procrastinators stand tall you have the qualifications to be a great leader. So, I say once again, go have some fun, be a procrastinator, never do today what you can put off until tomorrow.

The School

Bus

Marj Helmer

The School Bus

By Marj Helmer

It came around the corner. So big! And noisy. Black smoke puffed from its rear. It swayed and lumbered up the hill. I could see the driver. No jolly old elf he. His arms moved the wheel. His muscles bulged with the effort reminding me of Grandpa on his 1912 Harvester.

It hissed to a stop a little before our driveway. A quick hug and my boy climbed up the steps. My eyes washed my reality, but I couldn't allow any drops. His little sister was watching intently, cataloging the entire experience for her own first day of school in the future.

The bus driver looked everywhere but at my boy. I saw him in his blue cap, new backpack and sneakers as he paused at the top of the steps, peering down the aisle. Not one backward glance for us. Was there a seat for him? Did he know anyone? He moved into the bus and I saw him no more. He must have sat on the other side. There were other kids looking out at me. Mine was gone, into another world where I would only be allowed to visit.

The bus gears screeched and they lurched down the road. I waved and she copied me. She took my hand and led me up the drive toward the house.

Fake it
till You Find it

Mary Mitchell Lundeen

Fake it Till You Find it

By Mary Mitchell Lundeen

As I retired from my 35 year career, my mind wandered back to when I started my special education journey. Did I have a clue what was ahead? I was a naive young girl of eleven. My parish priest, a huge ex-football player with dark good looks and tons of personal charm, talked with me one day after Mass. He asked, "Would you like to go with me to Faribault State Hospital and work with the retarded?" The year was 1966 and *retarded* was the term being used. Some other of the cool and smart kids were going, including my friend Jeannie, so I said yes. We went over our four-day school break to a town a few hours away. I had no idea that this volunteer experience was to shape the rest of my adult life and give me passion in my career.

We arrived at the state hospital after sunset and, to my surprise, we were staying in the adult women's dorm. These retarded women were "high functioning" meaning they could talk and take care of themselves. They seem to be always smiling and I pretended that all was great with my limited interactions such as "good night" and "thank you" to each of them. I wasn't frightened of them but I did desire some distance. Couldn't I do God's work from across the room?? The big old brick building we were in was cold and without many decorations to make it a home. Of course, it

147

smelled like urine mixed with pine sol so you were reminded that someone wets their bed on a daily basis. That night, I tried my best to fall asleep in one of the old smelly beds. Instead, I lay awake thinking of something funny I was going to tell my brother: "No man is an island unless he wets the bed". Shouldn't I have spent my time praying like a good girl instead of thinking of silly potty jokes?? I better work hard at God's work tomorrow because I was faking this religious stuff most of the time.

I did an adequate job of making and faking my way through the next four days. Each volunteer had a building of their own to spend the daytime hours. My building was named Chippewa, a large brick men's building housing ninety men of various ages and IQ levels. At Chippewa, all the men could walk...one of the "sorting" criteria at this huge institution.

"Go right on in," said the front desk attendant, Bob, who was sitting inside the door of the massive structure. "Coffee is at 10:00." He must have read my hesitant stance at the open door. The room was as big as a school gymnasium with at least fifty adult men inside. Beyond the room, there were smaller rooms with dorm like beds. "Nobody is gonna hurt you. They love visitors! I am right here if you need me", Bob said with encouragement. I walked in only a few steps when at least ten men surrounded me and began touching my hair, arms, attempting to hug me. I felt suffocated and repulsed by the onslaught of body odor and dirty hands. Bob shooed them off of me saying "Hey, hey now.... let the little lady get her bearings. And no hugging". All of the men backed off a bit except for one. A fragile, tiny African American man kept touching my arm. I thought maybe he wanted to shake my hand. "Hi, I'm Mary" I offered with my hand outstretched. He mumbled back "Perry" and continued to hold tightly onto my arm. For the next four days, he stayed by my side touching my arm as often as possible as I made

148

the rounds. I figured Perry must have been one of those babies pushed out of the nest too soon without getting his needs met for love or comfort. Instead, he took my arm. Later, this would come to remind me of those early attachment experiments we watched in graduate school. My arm became a state hospital version of the wadded up cloth that the rhesus monkey clung to when abandoned by the mother monkey. Perry may not be able to get all of my attention, but he could have my arm.

My first impressions were that all of these men needed clothes that actually fit them. The clothes looked clean but the size was not a priority here. Loose fitting and short inseams were the mode o' day. Also, the five o'clock shadow was everywhere, a fashion trend forty years too soon. Teeth were crooked and yellow but smiles were abundant and genuine. Clearly, I had lucked out and got human beings who could interaction like preschoolers. But what did these men do all day? Some of the more clever ones had found a lifeline. Gary, a little bald Down syndrome guy, colored in coloring books all day with the concentration of a watchmaker - head bent down to focus intently. It made sense; because the crayons and books were something the hospital could easily keep on hand without spending much money. Gerald, a 60-year-old guy who seemed "normal" to me, raised rabbits out in the backyard. He cleaned the cages, held the rabbits, and made sure they had food. He said he was raised on a farm but his uncontrollable seizures landed him here. The farm was a dangerous place for someone with fits of falling. Wasn't there someplace else he could go? I was just beginning to understand that either you fit in the middle of the bell curve or you were an outlier. Those who do not fit in were at risk for all kinds of substandard living situations and loss of power.

Most of the men just wandered around the huge tile covered floor waiting for the next coffee break or meal. A TV was on in the corner and a piano was available. I played the piano and sang for several hours each day getting many voices to sing easy choruses such as "You are my sunshine" or "Row. Row, row your boat. " I was never much of a piano player but no one seemed to notice even prompting me to keep playing. One young man took on the role of a troublemaker, refusing to shower and then running away from the weary and underpaid staff attending to the daily routines. Thank god I only saw a flash of the nakedness... remember this is supposed to be God's work, not a free peek at the next mysteries of life. The coffee at 10:00 was weak and lukewarm served in stained beige institutional cups. Much like this whole situation, inadequate, but it could be called coffee. The same as this overall existence could be called living.

At lunch, I would go to see my holy and perfect friend Jeannie, who obviously was better at being here than I was. I felt uncomfortable and guarded most of the time. Jeannie would float among the cribs of the people in her building. She had the Linden building designed for those who lived their whole lives in cribs. A sea of forty cribs and Jeanne would glide from one to the next touching and cooing, rubbing and singing. I could hardly stand to peer in a crib afraid of the distortion of a human that I would see. People with heads as big as watermelons or eyes gooey and white. I admired Jeanne's ability to be comfortable with this and I told her so. I had to tell her this because I could hardly eat my lunch after seeing these crib beings. Jeanne was someone who knew how to do religion. I was clearly a pretender but this experience was providing me with an unsure path forward.

My four days ended with a sense that something important was here. Jeannie and I decided to make several

150

more trips to the state hospital. We would arrange our own visits throughout high school to keep up our volunteering. I was always happy to walk into Chippewa and gain Perry as an additional appendage for several days each year. I looked forward to seeing all my boys and spending time interacting with them, at whatever level they were at. I grew to know that somehow this was to be part of my future. I began to know that I was going to be a person that did things with and for other people. I could smile and chat. I could remember their names. I could take action to do things that made other people feel good like singing a favorite song or hanging a drawing. I could melt the ice with warm interactions. That is how I got my start in special education.

When I became a psychologist in my 20's, I reunited with Perry again when he was living in a group home in Golden Valley. I was so happy for him because he now had his own bedroom and a job at a nearby grocery store. He beamed as he held my arm in that old familiar way and showed me his space and stuff. This closure was very satisfying as I often wondered about Perry and my other boys.

I daydream back to my first exposure to the people at the state hospital. Remembering the discomfort, remembering that personal interactions helped make things better. I remembered how uncomfortable I was walking into my building Chippewa my first time when I was eleven. Later these outliers became my tribe. I gave a little smile, reflecting on lessons learned. Those long gone state hospital visits taught me that discomfort can shape one's path in surprising and satisfying ways.

A Walk with Gibbon McDern

M.M. Jayne

A Walk with Gibbon McDern

By M.M. Jayne

Change can well ruin you. My grandpaps said it every time I came home from college.

"I'm not ruined, Grandpaps. I'm learning."

He harrumphed from his tattered blue TV chair. I quietly closed the laptop, feeling slightly ashamed without knowing why. Everything Grandpaps said always had a ring of truth to it, but it was getting me down.

It was the summer after my freshman year of college. I came home to the ramshackle two-story house ten miles away from any town. You see a house like this, out in the middle of nowhere and think it was an old farmhouse, but there weren't any outbuildings, not even a single shed. The ten acres of land, wild and as falling down as the house, made up an island among the corn and bean fields of neighbor's properties.

I wasn't to know that this was grandpap's last summer on this earth, but it didn't matter. He'd been preparing to go at any minute since 1994. I was always about to give him a heart attack or be sorry when he got cancer. The specter of his death no longer sounded like a threat, but a sad promise. I loved him, but he got to be awfully tiresome at times. Now, with his hearing, he was still tiresome, but at volumes that could startle deer a mile away.

When I was young and full of wonder at the world around me, grandpaps was too. My mom always said having me put a spark of life back in her old dad. This was before the cancer took her. My pops remarried and we moved into town, leaving grandpaps out there by himself. When I was younger, I'd visit Grandpaps and we'd go out in the woods. He'd explain to me about moss and mushrooms and how a man died right here in the woods. I listened with rapt attention about Gibbon McDern, the escaped convict who hunkered down in the brush and trees, until the sheriff and his crew of deputies came upon him and shot him dead. Grandpaps would point out the spot in the woods by a weeping willow where Gibbon McDern tried to hide.

They say McDern shot a farmer while trying to get away with the man's daughter. The farmer died and McDern got 25 years in prison, swearing all the time that it was the girl who'd done the shooting. No one believed the girl was capable of such a thing, being the petite, pretty gal that she was. She kept her lips tight, allowing just a trickle of tear to roll down her face, so that the grown men stopped coming at her with their questions. Grandpaps snorted at his own re-telling, saying men are downright stupid when it comes to women. You don't know what they're capable of until you cross one.

When I was 15, I took Margaret Hanstead out to those woods to make out, only she didn't know that. I'd lured her out there with the wild stories of Gibbon McDern and she giggled nervously when I told her I could show her the place where he died in a hail of bullets. Grandpaps winked at me as we went out the door and to add a little atmosphere, yelled after us. "Don't make them ghosts mad." I could hear him cackling to himself right up until we crossed the wood line.

It worked for a bit. Margaret nervously reached for my hand and I quick rubbed the sweat off my palms onto my jeans and held her small, bony hand in mine. It wouldn't be the last time I'd scare a girl into giving me affection. The years ahead of haunted houses, dark swimming ponds, and tall tales that rendered hands and hugs and feels, started right there in the woods with Margaret.

The path that I'd threaded through the trees in years past was barely visible, as the woods began to reclaim itself from curious boys and cantankerous old men. Brush had reached out to hold hands with branches on the other side, combining to make the once familiar seem ominous. Grandpaps and I had been its only visitors for years, but when I went off to school and he couldn't be up for long without sitting down, the woods became a thing unto itself again.

This seemed like the moment to begin the narration that I'd been hearing since I could walk. I pushed aside branches and let Margaret pass. "Grandpaps said it was a bright June day. McDern had been four years in prison, so he was already a hardened man. He escaped off a farm where the convicts had been put to work bean walking. He just ran for a ditch when the shift warden was looking away. None of the other prisoners said boo. He ran and ran, hiding in sheds and farmhouses. Some say he was gunning for the girl and revenge." I glanced over at Margaret, feeling the grip of her hand tighten.

It wasn't long before I realized I was turned around and couldn't remember the direction of the infamous willow tree. Even if it didn't matter to Margaret, since she'd never know whether any old tree was the place of execution, it bothered me. We went further and further into the woods and she began to grumble. I was losing her attention and getting a little tired myself. I'd have to come up with something quick.

"Here's where the sheriff and his posse of men found McDern's shoes. They were muddy and waterlogged, so he just continued on barefoot. They didn't have the dogs with them, since they'd been loaned out a county over to find a missing kid. The sheriff figured McDern couldn't have gotten far in his condition – being tired, hungry, and now barefoot."

"How long had he been on the run?"

Her question startled me, as she hadn't said much up to this point. "A few hours, but McDern was on foot, so he couldn't get that far. Some say he was given food and water and new clothes by some farmer's wife, but no one has ever fessed up to it. When they got to him, he wasn't in any prison clothes and they never found where he'd gotten rid of them."

Margaret could tell I was trying to gin up the tale, if the look on her face was any indicator.

"Did your family live in the house at the time?"

"My grandma Rose lived there with her parents. She died before I was born, but Grandpaps told me the family was off to town that day and that Grandma Rose had begged off, because she was getting ready for her state teacher's exam." Margaret's hand loosened a little on mine, so I stopped talking.

Grandpaps also told me that Grandma Rose hated going to town. She didn't really like to go out anywhere and was pretty much that way her whole life – most years, she just went to the schoolhouse down the road to teach a handful of kids during the week. Folks were clamoring to get her fired because she just stopped going to church, but then one day, she showed up with Grandpap's wedding ring on her finger, giving her just enough respectability to keep her job.

By the time my grandma quit teaching, the town had grown to the point that they built the school there and let the little one-room school in the country fall in on itself. A couple of years ago, some history-minded folks in town got the idea that they should put it back together. Some were even of the mind that it would be a tourist stop when people were visiting the county during the fair. Then others said that no one in their right mind would drive out in the middle of nowhere to see a little white school, so now it was just a pile of grayed lumber.

Margaret made a noise that sounded like irritation and I was tempted to take her back to the house. We could sit drinking lemonade while Grandpaps snored in his chair, a game show blaring from the television. Part of me was stubborn though - another character flaw I'd inherited from Grandpaps. I kept pushing forward through the overgrowth and I could feel the resistant tug of Margaret's hand, who was likely beginning to regret coming along.

During high school, we took a field trip to the university library to learn how to do research. I looked up the local papers on microfiche, but couldn't find the story. I was disappointed, because I just couldn't picture what McDern looked like and I wanted to see it in print. Grandpaps said the local paper office burned down in the 1970s and they lost a lot of their records, but he said he'd go up to the attic and dig through to see if he could find the old paper clippings. He kept forgetting to do it and soon I forgot to ask, especially when he got saddled with a cane and couldn't do stairs.

Grandpaps said McDern was a short man with hippy hair, but I knew that's how he described any man's hair longer than a buzz cut. I was surprised that he hadn't said anything about mine, since I hadn't once gotten a haircut since leaving home. McDern wouldn't have likely had hippie hair, since they would have shaved it all off and shoved him into a prison jumper.

Margaret began to protest, but I was sure we were getting closer. I was right. One more bend on the trail and there it was. The weeping willow where McDern took his last breath. We stood in silence for a moment, but even I had to admit it was a bit of a letdown. Perhaps my imagination was preoccupied by the bumps in Margaret's sweater, because when I'd been out here with Grandpaps, I could see McDern, barefooted and hunkered down against the tree's trunk. I could see the group of men advancing on him, shouting at him to hold still. Grandpaps said they didn't know who fired the first shot, but somebody jumped the gun and it made all the others unload their weapons in a frenzy of hopped-up fear. McDern could easily have been taken in, but get a group of men with guns on a tracking mission, somebody is going to get jumpy.

Grandpaps would say in a low voice, "He was shot 26 times by the time the last bullet was fired. County swept it under the rug. Officials told everyone that McDern had resisted and wouldn't stop running..." I looked up at Grandpaps as his voice trailed away. His rheumy eyes seemed more watery than usual. We sat silently on a log until he groaned his way to a standing position. "Best get on before it gets dark." We'd lumber back to the house in silence. Later, I'd hear him limp out to the porch, where he'd sit, looking out into the woods, as if he were expecting company.

Margaret tugged my hand. "Let's go back, I'm getting cold."

I sighed with disappointment. I never could tell the story like Grandpaps did and Margaret never did put out, but it was the last time I went to the woods and the last time I thought about Gibbon McDern for a very long time.

In fall, Grandpaps began to do poorly, so I dropped out for the semester and came home to look after him. A neighbor lady several acres over had been stopping in on him every few days, bringing him some home cooking and making sure he was upright. Then she slipped in the tub and broke her hip and my Grandpaps called me. He'd never done that before, since I always called him, so I knew it was serious.

I got into the habit of making him meals and helping him to the toilet, but I could feel his frail bones when he leaned against me and hear the faintness of his breath. I told him he needed to go to the doctor, but short of shooting him with a tranquilizer dart, he wasn't going to be moved. The last days, he spent most of his time in bed groaning and whispering nonsense. I was reading his favorite book to him, The Last of the Mohicans, a little each day before he'd fall asleep and begin whispering his nonsense, "Rose, my Rose, she knew. I just couldn't let him. I just couldn't let him." The last night, while sleeping in the old rocker next to his bed, I awoke to a raspy sound followed by silence. Grandpaps was gone.

Being his only living relative, the estate was left to me. There would be little to gain, except maybe from the sale of the land. Since it'd have to be cleared and cultivated, the neighbors had little interest. I was okay with the standstill in selling. It gave me time to start going room by room, boxing things up, hauling things away in Grandpap's old Chevy. I pulled down the stairs that led to the attic, wary of what I'd discover. Nobody had been up there for years. To my surprise, it was just dusty. The house had held out against bats and rodents. Piles of boxes, Christmas decorations, and broken toys littered the small, low-ceilinged room. I found a light pull, but had to replace the bulb before I could explore. For the next week, I'd spend a few hours every day just going through things.

In a dark recess of the attic, I found an unlocked ammo box, its green metal scratched and worn. Inside there wasn't a gun or ammo, just newspaper clippings and old photos. There was a picture of a young woman with an older couple. On the back it said "L to R, Rose with William and Esther." This was my grandma and her parents. Even in the black-and-white, you could see how pretty she was, with dark hair and eyes that would bore into a man's soul. No wonder Grandpaps had fallen for her. He always said she had bewitched him. "There was never a man who could look away from my Rose. No saying no to that woman." He sighed and changed the subject.

The newspaper clippings were a gold mine. Here, at long last, I got to look on the face of Gibbon McDern. It was disappointing, if truth be told. He looked like an average, ordinary man, not even that tall. In the news story, it confirmed what Grandpaps had told me, except he'd left out the fact that the farmer shot by Gibbon McDern was my great-grandfather, William Anderson.

The girl that McDern had tried to run off with was my Grandma Rose, Grandpaps' beloved. The next article showed a group of men grinning and posing with pistols and shotguns. *Sheriff and Deputies Kill Escaped Convict* read the headline. When I saw the tarnished badge at the bottom of the ammo box, I got a magnifying glass and looked at the picture again. There he was, Grandpaps, a young deputy with a solemn face that stood out among the grins.

These many years later, I could only piece together the rest of the story. But like Grandpaps, I learned to tell a tall tale well. The house has been remodeled, but the woods remain. My wife hates it when I tell the story, but now my son, who no longer toddles when he walks, looks at me with wide eyes when I tell him how his great-Grandpaps shot a man, because of the woman he loved. We walk down the path that I clear every spring, find that old scarred willow and sit on a log while I recount the tale of Gibbon McDern. The telling is a little different from Grandpap's, but I like to think he'd have enjoyed it nonetheless.

My
Time

Sybil Swanson

My Time

By Sybil Swanson

"So come with me, where dreams are born, and time is never planned. Just think of happy things, and your heart will fly on wings, forever, in Never Never Land!" – J.M. Barrie, **Peter Pan: Fairy Tales**

As a young girl I lay on my bed and dreamed dreams. Can I remember them now? No. But it was wonderful to lay there and look out the window and dream myself somewhere else, or as someone else. My dad called it daydreaming. I called it daydreaming too, but in a good way, not in the snarky way he meant it. It was a time where I didn't have to think about the punishment, or the consequences of my behavior. I could just think of another place, another time, another life. I spent a lot of time doing this, to my parents' annoyance. They called me lazy; I called me unmotivated. Maybe we were both correct.

That was then. This is now. Now is when I paint, letting it become all-consuming. Buying one canvas size, then finding another size on sale, of which I already have 7 or 8 or 20, then filling the guest bedroom with them and other things pertaining to my art. A tad obsessive? Maybe two tads obsessive. I've taken over the dining area and filled it with more things pertaining to my art. This includes a paint box so large it takes up half the table. A lazy-susan filled four levels high with mixed paints, which frequently tumble down. Then there are the brushes, water bottles, and other paraphernalia that goes with the art. This leaves just enough space for my computer and, if I have everything centered just right, there's enough room to place my dinner plate and water to the side when I eat. It shouldn't matter. I am only one and need only a little space, and my kitty eats on the floor.

As I paint, I tend to forget about the cleaning, the tidiness of my home. I forget about the calls I need to make, the appointments I need to set. All this gets done--eventually. This is my time. Some day, I might get it right and do all the things in balance. Naw, that isn't going to happen!

I'm retired and I take that seriously. Which means that it's my time and I can do what I want, when I want. Wow! It's so powerful, so empowering to say: I can do what I want, when I want. Such freedom. A luxury over all luxuries. Is it selfish? Sometimes, yes, but for the most part no. My children are grown and have their own lives and schedules. My grandchildren are scattered and have their own lives. I no longer work, so no boss to please. Basically, there is no one I must answer to, no one I have to please most days; just myself and God, to whom I am most grateful. He has given me this time to reflect, to live the day I have, to dream, to plan or not to plan, to enjoy each day. What a gift to have my time. Thank you, God, thank you.

October by Marj Helmer

I drift through the round-a-bout in my copper HHR, slipping to the right to exit at Central. Freed of the vortex, my little derby, my "Pumpkin," rolls along, chasing the drying leaves into the air. Some reach up to the sky, a crisp blue, that reflects my thoughts.

I am heading to the lake. It's the close-up weekend. I don't know who else will show up. But I know the dock has to come out, the boat housed, the water drained and the toilet "anti-freeze."

I love raking the leaves. Not an easy job with all the trees. But I will fall into a great pile of molding, drying glory and burry myself until a rake calls me out.

October by Mary Mitchell Lundeen

I love having campfires in the cool evenings of October. A few good friends, some adult beverages, and a crackling fire combine to produce unforgettable experiences. Of course, the alcohol helps, but there is magic in gathering around the warmth and light of a fire. Cells phone stay in pockets and the age old skill of human communication takes over. Fire provides an ever changing centerpiece of flames, smoke and embers. As the evening rolls on, the dark sky deepens creating a cocoon of safety within the circle. Faces are illuminated with the soft reflection of the fire. The unique setting provides the opportunity for friends to be truly intimate. I have laughed until I cried and cried until I laughed at these moments. I am such a sucker for fires I even watch the television yule log at Christmas time, but it is not the same. It is the cool evenings of October that contain the magic.

October by Sybil Swanson

The Pretty Month

October is the month when the trees change clothes, and personalities. The leaves of the trees switch gowns from lush green to yummy yellow, glorious gold, rusty red and to blustery brown. Individually they are striking, beautiful in their finery, but combined the leaves are a symphony, calling out to all to come see, come jump into the mounds that have fallen and have some fun. Now, come and rake me up...I'm finished for the year. It's my last hurrah...until next spring.

The trees then show off their skeletons. Down to their bare bones. Some are gnarly, even scary. Some are sleek and slim, some seemingly perfect with their uplifted arms, others are broken yet have a beauty all their own. Yes, trees are a living thing. In fact, a little like people don't you think?

October by M.M. Jayne

October is my grandfather's month – the month of his birth, the month he married his second wife – my grandmother. October is when he got serious about his beloved Kansas City Chiefs each year, leaning into the television with his matching hat and sweatshirt. He was an old school gentleman with all the privilege and prejudice of his middle-class upbringing, but unerringly kind - and remarkably even-tempered in a family where men had not fared well.

Over the years, I'd trek from wherever I was to visit my grandparents. The visits were a constant and for this reason, a comfort to me during my rambling years. My grandpa would pull out his tape cassette player each time, beckon to me, and say "Listen to this, kiddo". He had taped his favorite big bands and dubbed in like a DJ. *That was the King of Swing, Benny Goodman. Coming up next, an oldie but goodie by Glenn Miller.* He'd start tapping his foot and snapping his finger to the rhythm, lost in a time when he didn't need afternoon naps or to be told to take his medicine.

We disagreed on politics and discussed history. His bookshelves were lined with military histories and there were coffee table books full of ships and weapons. He never failed to catch errors in World War II movies -an insignia placed wrong, the wrong kind of bayonet. I'd grin and bear his insistence, unable to argue on the technicalities.

Nearly 20 years ago he walked me down the aisle. 12 years ago, he bounced my chattering toddler on his knee. Nine years ago, he died after a series of strokes. October will always be his month. And every year, I put on some big band music and hear his voice. *Listen to this, kiddo.*

There's no room inside the box, so . . .

Marj Helmer, Editor

About In the Box Writing Pieces

When we first came together, we had to figure out what we wanted, needed to do. We had many levels of skill. Many had taken classes before. "The Loft," a regional writing center in downtown Minneapolis, Minnesota, was a common denominator. We reference classes, conferences, teachers. This gives us a basis to converse on writing and we all contribute materials and discussion of methods, definitions, referrals, and share what we hear and read. We plan to invite experts in writing, publishing, marketing, all facets of writing.

Most of us had worked with "prompts." So we did too. It was awkward. Marj had a book, but the prompts were too wordy and slushy. "Why do you write?" "What is the scariest, most important, romantic, silliest thing that ever happened to you?" "October." "Winter." Yes, we were writing, but not "WRITING." You know, character, plot, action, description.

Enter Michelle and her magic box* full of little cards in two colors, gold cards describe a character and copper are plot bits. We pull one of each color. We give ourselves

173

twenty minutes, and then we each read what we have written. No shyness allowed. It is amazing! We are amazing! We all write something. Nobody writes the same story. We all read. We all applaud each piece. We have a great time.

Lise, one of our members, used the box for NANOWRIMO (National Novel Writing Month, each November.) Each day, she pulled two cards and wrote a short story. Every day! (Look for her short story collection.)

Following are three sets of prompts. "October" was pre-box. "Something in the wall" and "the Singer" are two box prompts, along with "Rescued child" and "Blood." Remember, twenty minutes, no editing. Read aloud. Have fun!

Marj Helmer, Editor

*The Storymatic® available at Amazon

In the Box

singer
&
wall

I'm a Singer, Not a Demolition Expert

By Sybil Swanson

"I'm a singer! I'm a singer, not a demolition expert", grumbled Charles. "What is wrong with these people, why should I be the one doing this? I haven't the time to practice my singing much less demolish this room. Sam and Shirley just don't understand what it takes to continue to be a singer at my age", he continued to rage to himself. "I think I will just put a hole in the wall with the sledgehammer and then tell them it's just too hard on me to continue to do it. Yes, I think that's the answer, play the too-old-for-this card," he thought.

"I wonder what dad is doing in the den", Shirley said to Sam as she continued to toss old magazines into the bag. "I really think he's unhappy being told to work on the den."

"Well, I kind of feel the same way," retorted Sam. "After all it was your grandfather, not mine, who passed and left all this junk to be dealt with; and now you want to remodel the kitchen, enlarging it to include the den. This is hard work for all of us."

"Don't be silly, Sam, this will be great for all of us. This house is perfect with the exception of the small kitchen. We'll get this done in a snap once we get this junk cleared out."

"Did you hear that, Shirley? I think your dad is singing. Incredible, he's doing hard labor and he's singing. Hey, Dad, what are you singing about? "

"Shirley, Sam, look at what I just found! I really believe it is the song my dad was composing years ago and complained that he lost it. He was so discouraged because he thought it was his masterpiece and he'd never be able to compose anything as beautiful as that again. In fact, now that I think about it, he never did compose another piece that was worth much. I remember it and I thought it was beautiful. Mom thought it was awful. I always thought she hid it from him, and now I see that's exactly what she did...she stuffed it into that hole that was behind their wedding picture!"

Singer in the Wall

By Lise Spence-Parsons

The house on the hill had always been a local curiosity. The kids in the town had been playing in it for as long as anyone could remember. It had sat empty since at least 1925. It was high up on the hill, overlooking the rest of the town. It's dark walls and dirty windows doing nothing to lighten it's mood. The roof was long gone in places and the holes had been patched in by various bird's nests.

The kids climbed up the hill, shouting back to each other, daring each to do things in the house when they got there. One daring another to walk the roof beams across the whole width of the house. Another suggesting that they should spend a few hours in the coal cellar. The bantering continued until they reached the house. As they approached, they noticed a van parked outside, the van was dark green with gold lettering on the side.

"Maggie - your Local Singer"

The boys walked up to the van and tried to open the drivers door. It was locked. One of the others tried to praise open the back doors, but they too were locked quite firmly.

Chris, the leader of the group spoke up, "Maggie? I don't

recall any Maggie being a singer around here. Let's go into the house and see if we can find her or something."

The other boys nodded and they made their way into the old broken down house.

"I'm going to explore the old kitchen area", one them called.

He went off into the old kitchen space and looked out of the broken window into the overgrown back yard. He bent down and opened one of the broken down cupboards. The hinges squeaked and the rotten shelves inside were barely holding together. The whole area smelt of mice and musty old belongings. The boy shuddered and stood back up. Suddenly, he heard a faint singing coming from a closed area in the kitchen. It was a faint singing, hardly audible, he called out to the others, but they did not hear him, so went on towards the noise to investigate. He followed the sound of the singing and it took him to a larder door that was firmly closed. He pulled on the handle and yanked it open. The door fell from it hinges and revealed a bricked up area, not a shelved area at all. He stood back and looked, this house was full of surprises. He tapped on the wall with his fist. He stopped and then he heard a faint tapping coming back. He tapped again and then stopped. Again his tapping was mirrored back to him. What on earth?

He again tried calling to the others, but they off somewhere else. Then he heard the singing again, but it was now coming from over where the sink used to be. He walked over to the half demolished sink and tried turning the old rusty tap on. The water spluttered out, he turned it off. The singing was getting louder and then the tap turned itself back on and then off. He was getting quite scared now, first the tapping being repeated and then the tap turning itself off and on. He spun around meaning to leave the kitchen and the house, calling out to the others he went back into the hallway. Where were the others? He called to them again, no answer. He went outside, they must be hiding in the coal cellar he thought. He opened the front door and stepped outside. They were gone!

The Singer in Paris

By Caroline Munro

Pierre stepped in from the Paris sidewalk and ducked through the old oak door of the apartments above. His footsteps echoed on the marble floor as he walked to the wrought iron elevator. Stepping inside he closed the door behind him and searched through the calling cards next to the elevator buttons for his teacher's name. "Madame Vieaux Peccate, Professor of opera and piano, lessons given. Etage quatre ." The elevator shuddered into life and Pierre began the accent.

"La, la,la,la, la la" Pierre began to warm up his vocal cords. Madame was an excellent teacher and it was difficult to get classes with her, she was in high demand at his Music school but she had no tolerance for time wasters.

He knocked on the thick wooden door, there was a large pile of unopened mail on the mat and a scrawny cat curled its tail around his leg and purred loudly as he waited.

"Entre' Pierre, the door is open".

Pierre managed to gently shake off the cat and picked up the mail as he entered the darkened apartment.

"Leave those on the side darling and come closer".

Pierre screwed his eyes up and tried to find his way into Madames salon.

"It's very dark in here shall I open a blind?"

"No, no darling, I have a terrible headache, come here, come here sit on the chaise lounge over here". Pierre stumbled his way towards her, knocking over a dried up aspidistra plant on his way.

"So sorry Madame, I'll put the plant over here".

"Wonderful darling, wonderful".

Pierre could now make out Madames features as his eyes adjusted to the darkness, she was clutching her forehead and lay back on another couch, dressed in a Chinese kimono with an embroidered shawl around her shoulders.

"I should have called and cancelled today, I'm so sorry. I'm afraid this headache has kept me indisposed all morning. It's the damned mice in the wall, there are hundreds of them I'm sure. They scratch and squeal, I can hear them climbing up the plaster and in the rafters of the roof. They are driving me crazy with their continual noise. I am a fragile creature and I don't know what to do".

"Madame have you told the concierge? Maybe they can send someone up to lay traps?"

"I would never let that philandering cheater in my apartment! Never again. I don't want him sniffing around here and looking for favors. No! Absolutely No!"

"There was a very hungry looking cat outside your door, maybe I should let it in to work for food".

"No! I'm allergic to cats, I hate the damn things. Whatever you do, Don't let it in!"

"Well Madame I'm at a loss to know what to suggest?

Maybe I could get you some traps to put around the apartment, the pharmacy probably has some poison too?"

Madame Vieaux Peccate slowly stood up to her full height and looking Sternly at Pierre declared. "Get out!! Leave me alone with my mice, we will make beautiful music together."

Singer at the State Fair

By Mary Mitchell Lundeen

As usual, the heat was oppressive as we walked our way around the state fair. We cooled off with a thick, creamy milkshake with enough weight watcher points to run my entire week. The smells of the state fair were so distinct: one minute a waft of grease indicating the hot deliciousness of a corn dog and the next minute the repelling smell of horse poop. Who doesn't love this kind of adventure?

We sat to rest our tired legs, get out of the massive crowd and listen to a singer in a small bandshell. The lady was dressed as a rock star from the 70s with high hair and leather jeans. She was belting out familiar disco tunes with a steady beat to make us all tap our toes in response. When she finished with her song, the crowd gave a loud round of applause. When this died down, even though the band had stopped, there was a noticeable beat continuing to emit from the back of the band shell. Pound, pound, pound as if the disco was continuing. The singer raised her hands in an "I Don't know" gesture and moved to look behind the wall. Soon she was followed out by a young man, obviously developmentally disabled, holding the singer's hand. He was small and bald, with his head tilted permanently to one side

185

and flashing a huge smile of crooked teeth. The singer indicated to the man to sit on the edge of the stage and he lowered himself hands first plopping down. He grinned out to the audience and then to the singer. The singer said, "This one is for you" as she pointed and winked at the young man. The singer began her rendition of "Staying Alive" by the BeeGees and the young man matched the beat exactly with both his upper body rocking and his open hand slapping the stage in perfect rhythm.

"Let's get a beer" I said to my husband. He nodded and said with a grin "Gotta love The Great MN Get Together!".

Singing While Dusting

By Marj Helmer

She was singing show tunes as she dusted the upstairs bedrooms. "I feel pretty, oh so pretty, as I'm dusting all of my shit. Oh so pretty, so why do I live in this pit?" "I am 70 going on eighty, people no longer see me, my hair is grey, my chins equal trey, but anyway what the hair." A pirouette brought her crashing right into the wall and onto the floor. She was dazed and what was worse she had spritzed her undies upon landing.

She just sat for a minute to catch her breath. Then she heard humming. It was coming from the wall. It was the same tune she had been dusting and dancing to. She put her ear on the wall, and yes, the wall was singing. The voice was dusky and rough. Not a man, or a woman. Certainly not a child. It was getting louder.

She started a new tune. "Whenever I feel afraid, I hold my head erect, and whistle a happy tune, so no one can suspect I'm afraid." Now the thing in the wall started whistling along with her. It was better at whistling than singing.

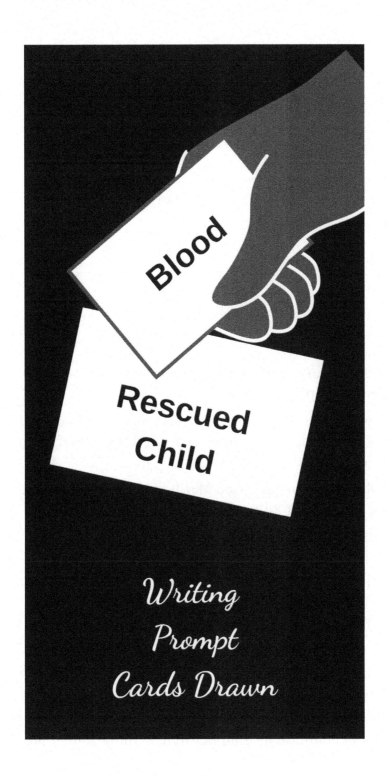

Writing
Prompt
Cards Drawn

Rescued Child with Blood One

By Sybil Swanson

"I don't want to go. no! no! You can't make me. Help someone, help!"

"I wonder what all that yelling is about," I asked Marilyn. "Why, it sounds like a child just around the corner from the Gap, let's go check it out."

"Oh my goodness," cried Marilyn. "That child is either being harassed or kidnapped. We must do something."

"But what?" I cried. "Oh, I know, I'm calling 911 right now, isn't that what they do on TV?"

"Oh, this is serious," whispered Marilyn. "See the man dragging her and then there are all the people just taking pictures with their phones, but not doing anything. Whatever is going on? No one seems to care but us."

"I've called 911 and told them there's a little girl being kidnapped. I hope that brings someone fast. At least mall security should arrive quickly, I would think."

"Don't count on it," said Marilyn. "I think sometimes they

just hide somewhere hoping the danger will go away without their showing up."

"I can't believe no one is stopping that baldheaded guy from dragging that child away. Let's do something, Marilyn."

"Hey, did you take a good look at him? He's bigger than John Wayne was for goodness sake. I certainly can't tackle him, nor could you. We'll just have to wait for the police."

"Well, I can't wait for the police, Marilyn. Hey, mister, leave that child alone! She can't go with you, she's supposed to come with me and...oh my goodness, she's bleeding! What have you done to her?

Stop! Leave her alone or ...or..."

"Stop! Cut!" Yelled a male voice from down the corridor. "Hey, lady, you just interrupted a great scene.

Get the hell out of here."

"What do you mean?" I asked.

"I mean for you to get out of this movie scene you have just ruined and cost us $100,000 dollars!"

"Oh dear! But I thought, I thought..."

"Yeah, well just mind your own damn business."

"Wait, Harry. This woman obviously thought something bad was going down. This is good news. It means the whole scene is believable after all. Thank you, mam. I'm Bruce Willis. Thanks for trying to be a good Samaritan and not just a gawker. Ok, Harry, let's get back to work! Maybe we should leave her chasing me down the hall in the scene, Harry. What a ya think?"

Rescued Child with Blood Two

By Caroline Munro

The police were used to these domestic disturbance calls. Times get rough in inner city Chicago. Gangs, poverty, lack of education. It was one big mixing pot of trouble and Hank Doherty was getting tired of it. Four more years and he would be out of it, retirement was Tantalizingly close. He day dreamed about relaxing, spending more time with family and friends, putting the stress of policing behind him. Not that he hadn't got satisfaction from his job, but the daily grind of dealing with what seemed like never ending trouble that just kept re- inventing itself got old fast. Hank had seen it all, he was ready to be done.

The squad car pulled up outside a typical inner city brownstone, in an area that time and money had forgotten. Now only the rats got fat and the once stately homes languished in disrepair and trash. Hank got out of the car and waited for his partner Doyle to join him. They had worked together in this neighborhood for going on ten years and had each other's back. It was like a work marriage. They liked to joke that they were a well-oiled machine and they knew each other better than their own wives did.

"Is this the right house? I can't see the number." Hank pulled the flashlight off his belt and aimed it at the door of the home. "Nothing here, no lights on indoors either."

"Who called it in Hank?"

"Passing dog walker"

"A bit late for dog walking this time of night?" Doyle shone his flashlight into the fenced front yard. "What a dump!" The light revealed an upturned shopping cart, old tires and beer cans strewn about on what once was a lawn.

Hank checked the mailbox by the front door. "This is the house, here's the number by the box. Doyle why don't you go around the back, just in case they do a runner."

Doyle took off, carefully picking through the yard trash.

Hank rapped on the door using the flashlight. "Police! Open up!" Silence. "This is the police, open up!" Nothing again. Hank made the decision to go in. He looked over the battered front door and decided that he could probably use his body weight to push it in. "I'm going in Doyle" he whispered into his radio.

With a loud grunt, Hank heaved his shoulder into the door and felt it give way. As he shone his flashlight into the gloom of the house he could smell the familiar sickly sweet scent of blood and he had a sinking feeling that they were too late on this call. He fumbled for a light switch and took a moment before switching it on and assessing the scene. Hank had been witness to a lot of murder scenes, he stored them away deep, never talked about them with his wife of friends, only his partner Doyle and the other officers shared the horror of a fresh murder and the dark depths of the human mind.

"In here Doyle! I've got two bodies."

"Calling in assistance," Doyle replied as he joined Hank in the living room.

Sitting in a battered, filthy armchair was a woman, slumped over. Blood splatter behind her, on the wall above the armchair and all over a crochet blanket that draped over the back of the chair.

"Looks like a gunshot to the head, not self-inflicted," Hank muttered half to himself.

Doyle was across the room looking at the second victim, a male lying face down on the floor, gunshot wound to the chest with a growing pool of blood around him.

"Try not to touch anything Doyle, I'm going to take a look around."

Carefully Hank walked around the rest of the ground floor with his gun at the ready. The kitchen was empty, he checked to see that no one was in the pantry. He stepped into what must have been a dining room once but was now filled with piles of trash and abandoned furniture, nothing there.

"I'm going up, do you wanna join me?"

Doyle fell in behind Hank and they quietly crept up the worn out carpeted stairs.

Hank pushed open the first door to a dark bedroom, Doyle followed on to the second door, another bedroom. But nothing, just silence. Two more doors remained closed. Hank indicated to Doyle to take the one at the end of the hallway and he slowly turned the handle on the last bedroom. Nothing there, just more trash and an old bed piled high with clothing. He returned to the hallway and followed Doyle into the last room. Doyle stood frozen to the spot, still holding his gun at the ready, pointing it at something on the floor. Hank stepped in behind him and peered into a murky, dark bathroom. A slither of light came in through the newspaper covered window. Just enough to illuminate a small figure, looked like a child, sitting in front of the bath. Knees pulled up tight, head down with skinny arms gripping a pistol out in front of it.

"Holy shit!!!" Hank cried. The child looked up, it was emaciated, hard to tell if it was a girl or boy because of the long greasy hair. Huge eyes stared up at them, haunted, with dark circles under them.

"We're not going to hurt you buddy. Everything's going to be ok. We're here to help," Hank whispered.

The child looked from Doyle to Hank and then back again to Doyle, Its lips curled back over its teeth and turned into a lopsided smile.

"BANG!!!!"

Works in Progress

We all have works in progress (WIP's). Remember saying "Someday I'll write a book," "That would make a great book", "I'm writing a book." I started my first novel in 1992. It began as a character sketch. Now it's 80,000 words and on its ninth revision. I've put it away and hauled it out again. I've pitched it to agents and had some positive responses. Still it waits. For what? For me.

The WIP's are just what they sound like, "whips." They are our masters. They haunt us. They call to us, "Listen to this, it would be great in your book." "Write this down, for your book." Oh, and those helpful supporters? "How's the book coming?" "Am I in it?" "What's it about?" I wish I had never told anyone.

But our "WIP's" are there. They are our "babies." Even if/when they are published, they will always be our "works in progress."

Marj Helmer, Editor

Mrs. A's

Tea

Party

Marj Helmer

Mrs. A's Tea Party

By Marj Helmer

"Mrs. A's Tea Party" is a review of abortion since the Roe v. Wade decision in 1976. In the style of "The Help" by Kathryn Stockett, three generations of women deal with unplanned pregnancies. Mrs. A takes is two pregnant teenagers, one her granddaughter. Unplanned pregnancies now have three outcomes. Adoption, parenting, and legal abortion. Times have indeed changed and lives must change too.

Chapter 1

There had been so many. Why did they keep coming? Tearing her apart with their problem. She helped them and stood by until it was over. They were around for a brief period and then got on with their lives. Mostly she lost track of them. But things were changing. There weren't as many coming now. Roe v Wade had made a difference. Now more options were available and women didn't have to be rich to have safe treatments and good care. Still they came for help, like Cheryl, who had appeared before the tea party, the pleas had been so simple.

"You helped so many, can't you help me?"

"Help you how, Cheryl?" Mrs. A responded. And waited.

"I can't go through with it! I can't face my friends! This is going to ruin everything! Crap!" She raced back and forth between the table and the door. Although racing was the wrong term for the short movements within the small kitchen space. She jerked around at each end of the race track, her young, fresh face flashing pain and terror.

Haunted. Scared. Fearful. Changing every minute. Cheryl kept cursing, her self-loathing causing the curses to come louder and more fiercely. Each time she got close to the door, Mrs. A thought she would yank it open and bolt. But what would she bolt to? Or, for that matter, from? The problem that brought her to the house that day was within her. There was no escape, not now, not ever. Mrs. A knew that even when Cheryl's problem was "solved," that problem was flesh of her flesh and indivisible from her.

Then, as she reached the door again, Cheryl turned and crashed against it, sliding to the floor. With her collapse, the cursing was replaced with sobs that were so violent, she beat her temples in order to make them stop, hoping the pain would give her control again.

Still Mrs. A waited. Cheryl calmed herself enough to stop the hitting. She banged her head several times back against the door. She began to take deep breaths. She wiped her eyes with the backs of her hands and her nose with the sleeve of her shirt.

Cheryl wasn't a pretty girl. She was tall and broad shouldered with some heft to her. Strong. Athletic. Not ugly, but not pretty. The ravages of her emotion had made her eyes red and swollen. Her skin was also red and blotchy. Her hair had come mostly out of the tight ponytail she wore. The mess actually made her more feminine, more fragile, more attractive. It softened her. Made her more sympathetic. Or was it that it made her only, after all, look vulnerable.

Mrs. A shifted in her chair. Cheryl looked up through the mess of her pain and anger. "I know you'll help either way," she said. "I've heard the talk."

Mrs. A waited, her eyes connected to the pleading face of the young girl. What did she want from her? Why did they keep coming to her? How had this all begun? What difference did it make? The only thing that mattered now was this drama in her kitchen. This young life "ruined," if she were to believe the woman before her.

For woman she was. She had been doing womanly things and her body had betrayed her. Her plans, her dreams, her hopes. Yes, even as young as she was, they were there. Plans, dreams, hopes. Ill formed or unformed, they were there.

"You know, I gotta play. I can't let the others down. I'm so tired." Cheryl shifted her anxious eyes to the floor. "All I do is cry. I can't be around anyone, 'cause they'll know. They'll ask. They're already on me about not being around. I tell 'em I'm anemic...."

"You probably are," Mrs. A interrupted. "Your body is meeting extra demands." But it wasn't time to speak yet. Cheryl was not listening.

"But they will know. And I can't have that. I can't lose. They'll hate me. I'm supposed to be the leader. They made me team captain. They look up to me. I can't do it! Can't do it! Oh God ...! Oh God." The last words were more like a moan than a prayer.

"And Kenny! He's such a kid. He has no idea. He is actually older, but he's such a kid. How could I ever...? Well, I did, obviously, or I wouldn't be here like this. Oh crap!" The anger was coming back, but she stopped it. She shook her head.

So much for Kenny. No help there. "Such a kid!" Mrs. A thought, things like this made adults out of kids. But Kenny wasn't going to know. Wasn't going to grow with Cheryl. Wasn't going to suffer. She almost added "the consequences." But she didn't need to. Suffer was right. Suffer and suffer and suffer. Cheryl would suffer. Kenny wouldn't. She might even continue with him. Her choice. She certainly seemed concerned with how things looked. So she might.

Cheryl was getting up. In a strong movement of her body, she reached her height, straightened her shoulders, grew a couple inches taller with resolution and came over to the table. Standing there, the fingers of her right hand lightly pressing the table surface, she said quietly, "Please help me.

.

The Remains of Men

Lise Spence-Parsons

The Remains of Men Book Introduction

Driven by her love of social history and its effects on people and their subsequent decisions, comes **Lise Spence-Parsons'** first novel, The Remains of Men.

It's the story of people lives across three independent eras of our recent history, how their lives intersect and drive the characters forward.

James, is a young man, born into abject poverty in the late nineteenth century, who follows a well-trodden path into World War One.

Robert, who also fought in the First World War, now finds himself living in middle upper-class relative security facing World War Two.

Charlotte, bright and bubbly and blissfully unaware of went before, runs around in the heady late 1990's media world in London.

The stories bring them all together and teach them all that no-one is immune to other people's thoughts and actions. James is driven by patriotic and family duty. Robert is ridden with guilt, anguish and will try anything to make it right. Charlotte learns that she has others that need her help to reconcile their lives.

The Remains

of Men

Sample Chapter

Lise Spence-Parsons

The Remains of Men
Sample Chapter

By Lise Spence-Parsons

November 1939

He stood under the street lamp on the corner of Caxton and Sterne Roads in Shepherd's Bush, London and watched the cigarette smoke swirl upwards into the night air. He could have made it turn out differently, but he'd chosen not to at the time. He turned, sighed and made his way back to the tube station and disappeared underground. It was time to go home.

He stood on the platform and waited patiently for a westbound central line tube to come screeching into the station, it was later than when he normally travelled home to Ealing Common and the tube that came into Shepherd's Bush had seats available. Doors opened with their normal hissing sound and he stepped inside the carriage, sat down next to another man reading the newspaper headlines. It seemed to Robert, that for the last couple of months it was all about Poland and Eastern Europe being annexed by Germany, Hitler already having claimed Austria as part of Germany. The tube rattled along the tracks in a darkness that matched his worries, that his sixteen-year-old son, John, could be called up if the war was prolonged. His daughter, Maisy was too young and anyway they were not calling up girls yet and he hoped that would never happen, it couldn't, could it? His thoughts swirled in his head as the tube came into Ealing Broadway. He got out, crossed to the other platform and waited for a train to take him one stop onto Ealing Common. He exited the station, tipping his hat to the station clerk taking tickets and walked wearily home, every one of his 52 years bearing down on him.

He turned into Warwick Road and trudged up to number 32, turning the key in the lock and calling out to his wife of 19 years, "Grace I'm home, sorry I'm late, I went for a walk by the market."

"That's fine darling" Grace answered, "dinner is in the oven, not very exciting I'm afraid, food is already becoming scarce."

Robert sat down at the kitchen table and began to eat his food, "how are the children? I worry so much about John and this war."

"They're both fine and doing their homework upstairs" Grace replied as she smoothed down her floral apron and pushed her blonde hair behind her ear.

"I've an early start tomorrow at the bank, think I will go to bed Grace."

Robert pushed his plate away and went upstairs, he was still brooding about his decision so many years ago. Grace sighed, picked up the plate and dumped it into the washing up bowl, she felt a slow tear trickle down her cheek, she tried to brush it way, but more fell quickly into the soapy water. She felt cheated by the war, the second war to impact her, she remembered the Great War all too clearly, how it took away loved ones, terrifying her to the core, knowing that it would happen all over again.

He woke up early, before the alarm clock rang, he slipped quietly out of bed so not to wake Grace and walked softly down the hallway into the bathroom, he sighed, yet another room that needed work. He loved living in Ealing, but it was expensive and although his bank job gave him good perks, it was difficult and not always enough money for renovations. Grace never moaned though, and she did her best to keep it all together. He washed, shaved and then with his robe on went back to his bedroom and quietly selected his formal bank attire for the day. He went downstairs, brewed coffee, it was getting scare so he really savored the taste.

He walked back down Warwick Street and reversed last night's tube trip back to Shepherd's Bush thinking about it all again, trying to resolve it in his mind. It did not matter how he looked at it, he knew that he'd been wrong, and he now regretted the decision, but on the other hand, he would not have what he had today if he'd chosen the other path. The tube finally got to Shepherd's Bush and he trudged down Frithwell Road and went into the bank.

"Morning Mary, can you get me the Baker's file and a cup of coffee please"

"Of course Mr Downs, they should be here in few minutes", Mary answered handing him the file.

He sat at this desk and read the file, he felt sorry for them, but there was nothing he could do, his hands were tied. It was hard all round and now the war compounding it further.

The morning passed quite quickly and he ate his plain, slightly dry sandwich whilst going over and over it in his mind, eventually making himself stop and get back to work. He knew he had to stop torturing himself. Robert had a busy afternoon with customer queries and loan requests to grant or deny, he looked at his pocket watch, his parents gave him on his twenty-first birthday way back in 1908, the Golden Years of endless summers and tennis matches. No-one then imagined the horrors that were to come dividing Europe and man alike and that it would be repeated a mere 21 years later. It was 5 o'clock, time to return home, the tube was busy this evening and he had to stand all the way home, squashed and hot. Just time to get home, change and then go out the Auxiliary Fire Service station and report for a night of street walking and black-out enforcement.

Abide-A-While

Resort

Marj Helmer

Abide-A-While Resort

By Marj Helmer

The Abide-A-While Resort is a review of "the end of life" issues we all face eventually and how or if we manage those issues. Do we seek treatment even though it may mean days, weeks, months of suffering? Do we "hang in there" for our loved ones? Do we go off by ourselves to spare others? Do we take our own lives to "be in charge" of the end?

Most of us won't need to deal with it. The end will come upon us and have it's way with us. Some of us will plan 'the end." The Abide-A-While resort is a hostel by the lake with caregivers and plans to help reach that end graciously, serenely, in community.

Chapter 1

His clients only come through referrals. That's the safest way. There are still so many who think that setting a limit to your life is wrong. They believe you have to live to the brutal end, suffer whatever the "powers that be" decide for you. But George has a vision. That's what it is.

He found a resort just south of the Canadian-Minnesota border. A run down "Mom and Pop" operation. On a peninsula on a private lake. He set up there in the middle of the woods. A couple cabins had to come down. But that just left more room between the remaining cabins. And because he planned on specializing, he figured he could start out small. There's room to grow into the woods, since most of his guests won't be using the lake.

213

Still, the Bide-a-While Resort has all the amenities. The swimming beach is sandy, not all that weedy. The dock is used for fishing, boats and sunning. It is in the shape of a "T" with two benches for sunrise and sunset viewing. Adirondack chairs in primary colors dot the beach and lawn. Picnic tables scatter about. The trees are tall and old. Pines, birches, poplars, oaks, maples. The shade they provide also generates dappled patches of light dancing across the grounds. The cabin roofs are shakes overtaken by moss. They add to the soft green light of the day. The windows are double hung with the small panes of glass that reflect the sunlight falling through the trees. The cabins close to the shore echo the lapping of the waves giving a softness to the sounds of the resort. The birds and squirrels keep a quiet existence. The paths are pea rock pushed into the dirt so bare feet can wander around the place. Quiet. Peaceful. Isolated. Almost a retreat.

George makes up the business as he goes along. A vision needs clarification and since his vision includes clients with different needs, he chooses to be flexible about the services he offers. He finds that the initial contact is best at a diner, café or coffee shop. At this first meeting, he has a brochure that shows the resort and talks about the "mission." But before he hands it out, he asks the client about friends, family, work. And why he called, what his needs are, where his life is. The health discussions come up quickly. Questions of diagnosis, prognosis, treatments. This is when the family's and friends' wishes come up. And after that, George always says, "And you? What are your wishes?" Often times the answer is "I don't know. I need to think about it." Then the brochure appears, and George explains that the Bide-a-While offers privacy and peace for just that kind of thinking. But he doesn't bring out the contract just then. He mentions his once a month gathering where prospective clients come for lunch, if they can, and learn more about the resort and its services.

So, the second contact is at his home in a first ring suburb. His assistant, Lisa, attends and helps with food, introductions and comments to keep the conversation going. Not everyone is in the same mode, but they are mostly in the same situation. To keep going or to call it quits? How long and when? How and where?

George lays out food on the kitchen counter and sample contracts on the sideboard. These contracts don't mention health. They list services provided by the resort. Housekeeping, grocery delivery, laundry, personal care, medical service needs, medication needs. They determine if visits are desired. Or a phone, WiFi, newspaper delivery, mail, pets, heat or air conditioning, boat or ice house. Or maybe a partner to stay also. But the partners have to sign the part of the contract stating they agree and acknowledge the wishes expressed in the contact and will abide with the client's desires. Each service adds a little to the basic rent which is charged on a weekly basis. Not unlike the assisted living places popping up all over for the baby boomers. Only the contract is not for assisted living.

There is no place for insurance in George's business. The contract is between the client and Life Vision, Inc., which is the name of the business and the corporation that owns the Bide-a-While Resort. The clients seem willing to pay their own way and thereby maintain control of their lives. There's no slippery slide to nursing home and hospice care decided by the insurance company executives.

Currently he is all booked through the end of July. Five cabins, five guests. Sarah, John, Ed, Frank, and Immanuel. He always insists on real names and photo id's for contracts, but aliases are used at the resort if that is what is desired.

Sarah, the only woman at Bide-a-While this week, is 82

and has congestive heart failure. She gets around on good days with a cane and on other days with a power wheelchair. She contracted for weekly laundry, housecleaning, and two meals a day, brunch and dinner. Air conditioning, Pookie's special dog food and chews, dog walking and poop pickup. She gets satellite TV and still has her cell phone. She likes a radio going, mostly all night. She visits with staff and Frank in Cabin 3. She and Frank play gin rummy at the picnic table.

John contracted for the cabin only. Cabin number 4. He moved in with only one suitcase. He loves to walk in the woods. He sits outside by his front door if he isn't out walking, but never speaks. He looks like he would only growl anyways.

Ed has been there for quite a while. Nobody goes to his cabin. And nobody comes out. None of the others can remember seeing him. Well, it isn't really correct to say no one. The resort manager, has been going in once a day the last week. He uses a key to enter and locks up when he leaves. For a few days, there had been moans floating around the cabin, but they all ignored them as they had agreed in their contracts. And the noises had stopped Tuesday.

Frank. Well, we know he plays cards with Sarah at the picnic table. Not every day. Weather gets involved. If she doesn't go to the picnic table, neither does he. But it is something he will do. And she is company enough. Frank has a contract for three months. He has food, beverage, air conditioning, TV, library access, guitar lessons (he has been playing for ten years now), dishwashing, laundry, and housekeeping. He is starting to feel like he is on vacation. His last day is the day after tomorrow.

Immanuel is young. Not relatively speaking, but really young. Like thirty, thirty five. Young. And handsome.

Really. Like Brad Pitt. No one sees much of him either. Maybe a glimpse at the window. Or a shadow next to the open door. His services are the normal services. The daily necessities. He has only been there for the one week. Staff comes and goes, but no contact with the other guests yet

Magpies'
Treasure

Caroline Munro

Magpies' Treasure

By Caroline Munro

The Magpies swooped out of the oak tree and caught the
strong current of wind that carried them towards the city of
Winchester. They squawked to each other in excitement as
they flew over the chimneys, rooftops and spires of the
Cathedral. Victor was the King of the Magpies and the
younger magpies were eager to learn his skills of treasure
hunting in the busy streets of the city. Victor had been in
search of something shiny to decorate the nest he and his
wife Eliza had been building. He wanted it to be the finest,
shiniest and most eye catching nest in all of the woods. He
had built it high in the oldest oak tree he could find, looking
down on the city of Winchester. He hoped it would be safe
from predators wanting to eat his eggs, or worse still, a

219

jealous competitor who might want to steal his treasures Victor was constantly moving and arranging his shiny bits of glass, silver or gold he had "borrowed" from the people of the city. He didn't see it as stealing, the items he found were discarded in the street, found in piles of rubbish or forgotten by a distracted shopper in the market. The younger magpies envied his daring and agility as he "picked" his way through the alleyways, markets and gardens.

Today Victor was determined to remove the object of his deepest desire, a silver cup that was attached to a chain in a college courtyard. It was proving to be a challenge to unpick the chain and release the shiny cup from the wall. Normally Victor liked to scavenge on his own but today he had to engage the help of his strong young friends. As they flew over the cathedral rooftop, Victor guided them down College street, under the college archway into the cobbled courtyard. Over to the right, attached to the wall was the silver cup glinting in the sunlight. The younger Magpies screeched and attacked the chain with their sharp beaks. Feathers flew and their talons caught in the chain as they struggled to be the first to release the cup. The Head porter Charlie who lived in the gatehouse heard the terrible noise and came out shouting and waving his broom to scare them off, but it was too late. With one last tug Victor claimed his prize and fled from the courtyard closely followed by the excited younger magpies. Their happy cries echoed around the courtyard as Charlie the porter stared in disbelief at the loose chain. How was he going to explain this theft to the college and what on earth could he do to get it back?

An Untitled Book

About a Child With Callous Unemotional Traits

Mary Mitchell Lundeen

An Untitled Book About a Child with Callous Unemotional Traits

By Mary Mitchell Lundeen

The tiny baby was wailing incessantly in the back seat of the car. The crying baby was in a rear-facing car seat. The worried mother was driving as fast as she could while she stole glances in the rearview mirror straining to see what was wrong. She was producing a stream of soothing motherese: "We are almost home; it is OK. Mom loves you. You must be hungry. Big brother Aaron is back there with you. Oh sweetie, sweetie." Mom was also giving orders to the older brother, Aaron, who was in the back seat. "Can you give him his pacifier?" and "Can you hold his hand?" Mom was speeding twenty miles over the speed limit towards home, which was just a mile away.

The tension was as high as the irritating wailing. All of a sudden, the baby stopped crying. The car engine could be heard as well as the radio. "Oh, thank God!" exclaimed the frantic Mom. She turned into the driveway, flew out of her seat and opened the back door. Aaron had one shoe on and his other foot hung bare from his car seat position. Aaron was smiling in an oddly satisfied way. Mom then looked at the baby. The baby had Aaron's sock hanging from his mouth and was writhing and gasping for breath with wide, panicked eyes. It took a couple of seconds to sink in. How did the sock get in the baby's mouth?....oh wait.....("Aaron, WHAT DID YOU DO?" shrieked his incredulous Mom.

Scampering

Around

the West

Year One

David Zander

Scampering Around Out West Year One

Retirement means discovering new tribes

The RV lifestyle

A question facing many retirees and widowers is what I am going to do with the rest of my life. I had worked until 2010, retired at age 70. The question was made even more perplexing by the unexpected loss of my lovely wife and life adventurer Kathy. Kathy died unexpectedly from lung cancer in 2014. And now I was alone, and 77.

This memoir is the story of my retirement and adventures. It includes the story of traveling with a RV. But it is also the story of coping with life after death of one's partner.

In May of 2017 I became the owner of a Scamp RV. I joked with my grief group by telling them I had a new relationship, pausing, noting how the group of widows and widowers had gone strangely still and quiet. Then I reached into my bag and said "I have a photo of her." Sounds of laughter, tension release as I brought out a brochure about Scamp RVs and said, "We are already sleeping together."

Scamp at Birch Bay RV Park, Agate Lake,
Nisswa, Minnesota

That first day of ownership, I towed my Scamp from Backus down to Agate Lake, just west of the larger Gull Lake. I had intended to be in that area all summer, learning about RV life before going off on any longer trips. And there was a lot to learn. I met Tom, my neighbor in the site next to mine on the lakeshore. Tom had travelled 26,000 miles solo, in his Diesel RV, down through North Carolina, and even into Mexico. It was not exactly a feeling of competition, but Tom was the inspiration I needed to go on a longer road trip. I had one destination on my bucket list, Crater Lake, Oregon. And so after two months in Minnesota, I set off with my dog Finn on our trip out west.

The inspiration to see Crater Lake lay with another source of inspiration, the Minnesota writer Cheryl Stayed. I read her book Wildland saw the movie about her backpacking on the Pacific Coast. It was from her that I first learned about Crater Lake. I have an impetuous streak. Based solely on this I decided to go see this wonder of the world. I had decided to head northwest on Highway 10 to Moorhead and take a North Dakota route west across North Dakota. I no idea how far I would get that first evening. Towards sunset I decided to test out a theory. It was said you could park overnight for free in Walmart parking lots. My GPS maps on my iPhone directed me to the Moorhead Walmart and yes there were about seven RVs clustered together in the large parking lot. I choose a space next to a clump of bushes where Finn could pee, made a hot cocoa and settled in for the night. The next day I drove west on I94 to Bismarck. The road was not busy. Disgraceful! Three of the rest stops were closed!

On My Way but do I really know where I am going, and why, and how to get there? And what will I find?

Where are we going? I don't know. When will we be there? I ain't certain.

All I know is I am on my way. (From the musical Paint Your Wagon)

Crater Lake

August 10, 2017: It's a sunny warm afternoon. There is no forest fire smoke in the air. I am sitting with Finn on the dog friendly narrow strip of terrace at Crater Lake Lodge, high in the mountains of Southern Oregon, enjoying the view out over the deep blue lake while sipping tea. I felt a feeling of bliss. It has taken a week to get here, about 1800 miles from Mpls. It is said that the human species has a drive to explore. I have followed the call of this this drive and reached my destination. The lake is stretched out before me.

I had left my Scamp about thirty miles away at a lower altitude in Wally's RV Park in the national forest near Chiloquin. A good decision. The last seven miles up to the

227

crater were a curving climb of steep gradients, sharp bends, and no guard rails; just suicidal plunging drop offs from a narrow shoulder edging the two way road. My wife Kathy would not have liked this mountain ascent. She would have been screaming.

I followed the rim road circling the crater and stopped frequently at the many viewpoints. Finn and I looked down at the Wizard Island and at the Phantom Ship visible only from some of the look outs.

Crater Lake *(and the wonders of the iPhone camera).

I stopped at the visitor center and watched a video that startled me with geological history. I had assumed that Crater Lake was formed millions of years ago but it has only been 7,700 years since the pressure from magna under the volcano expelled it off the crust of the earth and left a crater which then slowly over seven centuries filled with melting snows. I purchased one book of local legends. It detailed the stories of that have been handed down in the myths of the local Native American tribes. They tell of a mountain god who wanted to marry the local daughter of a chief. When she refused him, he exploded with rage. The elders sacrificed themselves to restore peace in the region. Like many mountain lakes this one has been stocked with fish by local fishermen.

After an hour or so at the terrace, and conversations with two sisters visiting from Kansas City who wanted to pet Finn, I took my folding chair from the car, found a quiet shady viewpoint and spent some time in mindfulness meditation, just being there, no thoughts, just dwelling in the peace and serenity of this majestic view born out of earth shattering, magna spewed, violence. Could it happen again? Undoubtedly! Seven thousand years is just the blink of an eye to these underground forces. But an extraordinary beauty resulted. Nature is a savage creator.

It seemed eons since I had left on my trip. I felt different. I felt very different from the person I had been back in Idaho, Wyoming, and Montana. Yet that was only a few days ago. A subtle psychological transformation seemed to have occurred when I turned south from Burns and drove across the high desert. I was totally alone in an alien environment. Open range. Having to carefully pay attention to fuel gauges. But I was succeeding. I felt like a knight on a quest of the Holy Grail, yet this was no small chalice, this was a huge cup of water formed by nature and I was almost there. And nothing bad happened. No flat tires, no engine breakdowns. I had taken precautions to get the vehicle in top running order, like a knight his horse. If I had not ventured out on this adventure I could sense how I would have remained in a darker, depressed, bored, mental state, like one of those Victorian widows shrouded in black who never emerged from their grief and sorrow. But here was a wide, new open horizon. I was following this inner drive to explore the planet.

My Scamp at Wally's RV Park

Onward to the Pacific Ocean

My original intention after Crater Lake had been to take a route back through Colorado and visit Kathy's uncle in Denver. But he was off on a trip of his own. As I studied maps I realized the Pacific coastline was only two hundred miles away. People were also suggesting that if U went just a few miles south of the Californian Oregon border I could see the Redwood trees.

When I talked to Gail, the owner of Wally's RV Park, about passes through the mountains, she wrote out some directions for a beautiful backcountry route over to Grants Pass. From there I dropped down into wine vineyards. I spent another blissful hour tasting wines at Longsword Winery. It was a bucolic scene of geese wandering around and sheep enjoying the fruits of labor of the owners. I have one of their bottles of wine from their vineyard.

I did not yet have a reservation for that night but I noticed an attractive RV camp on the main highway in the area of the Redwoods. It was about five p.m. I drove into the V Park, found the office, and they had a vacancy. This became a pattern for many days on the route back. I would start looking for an RV Park mid-afternoon, using an app on my iPhone, and make a call. I found reservations.

The Staff at %Redwood Meadows RV told me routes to take nearby in the redwood forests but that it would be best to unhitch the Scamp and just take my car, After some hours spent with Finn in the magical aura of the trees, we went back to the RV park, hitched up Scamp and drove to Hwy 101 and then north into Oregon and up to Gold Beach.

The rocks along the Oregon coast line filled me with awe.

I had called ahead to Gold Beach RV Park to make a reservation. It was a very small RV park just off the main high-street, near a bookstore and an ACE hardware store. I walked down to the local ACE hardware store. There was a small dog wandering the isles. He had a delightful harness that avoided any tugs on his neck from a leash. I brought Finn into the store and he was outfitted with a wonderful blue harness with a matching blue leash. We also added to his supplies with a large bag of grain free c treats.

I asked the staff what was their favorite restaurant and they directed me to a perfect choice where I sat at the bar and had local fish and chips and clam chowder. Another guy seated at the bar told me he had caught an 18 pound salmon out in the bay.

The next day I drove up to North Bend and encountered a new subgroup of the RV tribe. The office staff warned me that there would be lots of ATVs there. This did not perturb me from going there. The ATVs were there because this RV was a mecca for sand dune enthusiasts. I saw children as young as ten years old going off solo on their mini ATVs into the dunes. By daylight the ATVs sported a long red flag. One of the most beautiful sights was in the evening dusk; I saw a couple leaving for the dunes with long neon rainbow lights. It transformed from a noisy macho materialist mechanical scene. It seemed magical. The sand dune riders made me think of how the snow mobilers enjoy the Minnesota winters.

The next day I drove further north up the coast to the delightful town of Florence, Oregon. North of Florence I discovered the charming tiny town of Yachats, twelve miles north of Florence. We hiked up to the Heceta Head Lighthouse and sat listening to the waves below. I visited the sea lion caves. Finn and I spent many hours out on long beaches. He seemed to really enjoy all the sea shore smells of the ocean. I was worried about him getting sick from drinking salt water. But it did not become a problem. I always had water for Jinn in the car. Here is one of my favorite photos. Like Travels with Charlie, I had Finn my loyal companion. A reason for having the Scamp was so that I would not leave Finn behind.

There was another challenge looming on the horizon. The solar eclipse was forecast for August 21, 2017. There were rumors and reports of crowded freeways and traffic jams and gas stations running out of fuel. When I reached Heceta Beach, Florence, Oregon, I decided to stay put and was able to extend my two night reservation and stay to five nights. So that was partly the reason why for the next day Finn and I left the Scamp in the RV Park and I drove north to sea lion caves and lighthouses and deserted beaches. I will not forget Finn and me scrambling down over rocks and then taking off his leash so he could run out and explore the long beaches. I look at Finn and can see Finn running on hard sand sniffing all the beach smells. He was a very happy dog. I had more delicious sea food meals at numerous restaurants in old town Florence and at the driftwood inn in the beautiful coastal town of Yachats. Few people around but crowded memories.

Finn explores the sea shore on a beach north of Yachats in Oregon

Solar Eclipse on the Oregon Coast

My friend Wayne was the first to alert me about a problem finding space in RV camps due to the solar eclipse. He had seen an article that thousands of RV owners were heading to Idaho and Nebraska in their RVs to see the solar eclipse and that finding a space in an RV park would be difficult. All the RV parks on my route back would be filled. There would be no vacancies. I began to see articles in the tourist information centers. . Idaho Falls was planning a big festival. I noticed solar eclipse themes on t shirts for Sites along the path of the solar eclipse; including Florence and Yachats. I had not decided how or where I was going to view the event. I arrived in Hecate beach and decided to stay put. There were rumors of huge traffic jams on the freeways, gas stations running out of gas

Things have been a little spooky these last few years since Kathy died. Startling synchronicities frequently occur. The one I want to describe here is about how I spent the solar eclipse, unplanned but strangely appropriate. At the turnoff from Hwy 101 to Heceta Beach Road leading to the RV Park there was a small parade of shops. I stopped in at the grocery store and looked at the other businesses. Nestled in these, in a plain shop front was the Florence Unitarian Universalist Fellowship. A small sign on the door told me they hold their Sunday fellowship meeting there at ten am. I decided to attend. The Unitarian Universalists practice in a spiritual way l I feel comfortable with.

On Sunday August 20th, I went to the fellowship meeting. The Unitarian Universalist was about a mile from the RV Park. What to wear? I felt I should not wear jeans but I needed not to have worried, the casual clothes I wore were fine. The service offered a time for reflection and instead of a sermon from a minister there was a speaker on a social environmental issue, the crop dusting using chemicals.

In an announcements section, someone mentioned the eclipse and said that a group was gathering at the labyrinth. It was an open invitation. I was given some directions to the place of the labyrinth. It was on the grounds of another church in Florence. The next morning, the morning of the eclipse, I left my Scamp at the RV Park and drove to St Andrew's Episcopal Church. I was the first to arrive. There was no one there. I looked at a sheet of directions for entering the labyrinth and began my solo ritual.

Entering the labyrinth Guidance and instructions.

Choose a question enter the labyrinth

A meditative state I was alone in the labyrinth the first to arrive

I took Kathy into the labyrinth and had my own private memorial. Other people arrived when I was sitting mediating in the center of the labyrinth. Finn was in the car.

The group had their own strange rituals and dance. It included drawing a card from a wisdom deck of cards. I drew one card from the wisdom deck. It had hawk on it and spoke to the theme of release. It was very appropriate. I had felt that my experience in the labyrinth was about release. My sadness was in the three years up to going into the maze. The meaning for me now was to go forward in life not carrying this burden of grief. I would always love Kathy. She was here with me deep in my heart. But I felt a release of dark sadness and sorrow. It was time to go forward. I had faced fears travelling out alone and met great people, and felt awed by nature.

My journey back brought me across an ever changing landscape. The beauty of misty peaks in the mountains frequently brought tears to my eyes. Scampering around has been my way of letting go of sorrow.

Scampering

Around

the West

Year Two

David Zander

Scampering Around the West Year Two

By David Zander

Scampering Out West Year Two (2018): In the footsteps of Basho

Driving along a twisting stretch of road in Montana I suddenly crested an incline and the horizon ahead was filled with snowcapped mountains. I was filled with awe. A few days later seated on a bus on the Going to the Sun Road in Glacier National Park a mountain sheep suddenly appeared just yards from where I was sitting. It walked across the road in front of the stationary bus then leapt deftly over the rocks and disappeared down into a V shaped glarier valley. Again I was in awe. I named him Houdini.

Since my return from Montana my writing has unexpectedly veered off into a new terrain, new genres. It came about when I was reading "What light can do: essays on art, imagination and the natural world" by Richard Hass. In one essay, writing about Emily Dickinson, Hass suddenly compared her to Basho. It was like finding a faint trail marked with piles of stones. The trail led me to Richard Hass's translations '*The Essential Haiku: versions of Basho, Buson and Issa.* I read a copy of Basho's Narrow Road to the Northern Provinces with his journals and notes on nature writing. I should also mention that for the last four years I have been practicing Mindfulness meditation with teachers at a Zen center. One of Basho's poems had a very powerful effect on me. There are many translations. But I like this one:

An old pond

Frog jumps in

Sound of water

Basho wrote this haiku four hundred years ago. A Zen monk, on a pilgrimage, Basho sat quietly with his ink brushes fully aware of his environment, in the here and now. The poem, using two senses, expresses what he saw and heard. There are perhaps many levels of meaning and associations to this poem. For me it solved a problem. It showed me how to write in a way that captured intense experiences I had had on my narrow road to the Northern provinces, my journey out to Glacier Park Montana.

I don't think I have ever thought deeply about a philosophy for my writing. But Basho provided me with one in the notes he left on how to write nature poems in an essay called Learning from the Pine. For me his approach embodies mindfulness meditation with one's full focus on what you are writing about.

One must first of all concentrate one's thoughts on the object. Once one's mind achieves a state of concentration and the space between oneself and the object disappears, the essential nature of the object can be perceived. Then express it immediately. If one ponders it, it will vanish from the mind.

'Quickly say what is in your mind; never hesitate a moment. Composition must occur in an instant.'

Basho said make the universe your companion, always bearing in mind the true nature of things – mountains and rivers, trees and grasses, and humanity – and enjoy the falling blossoms and the scattering leaves. Here are some examples of how I have been applying this philosophy to my writing:

On

Zen

Poetry

David Zander

Zen Poems

By David Zander

The lake grows dark cold
Far off the sound of a loon
Faintly dabs at night.

It brings together all the rains and melting snow
The Mississippi our great river
And returns them all to the sea.

All night they gossip
Sandhill cranes on the Platte River
Gathering each spring

Winding stretch of road
Suddenly snowcapped mountains
Sight fills me with awe.

Winding gravel path
A small green snake
We stare at each other.

So precarious
Spider your web on my gate
But what can I do?

Cicadas whine
Crows caw, robins flap their wings
Summer symphony

At the sound of rain
Sunflowers open their round yellow eyes

Sun light wakes up my garden

A mother duck crossing a road
Her fledglings bunched tight by her tail –
I hold my breath in fear for their safety

Another year gone
Worn-out sandals on my feet
Grief still in my heart

Biographies

*We are what
we are,
so celebrate!*

Biographies

We are what we are,

so celebrate!

Sarah Bromage

I was born in the United Kingdom and spent the first 64 years there with a break in France for 18 months and Norway another 18 months with three months in Russia. Rather without too much thought but quite a lot of planning we found ourselves living here in Minnesota for another of our adventures. Moving to America has been as if I have started a new book (very strange and new characters and attitude to life) then slowly realizing how much I am enjoying this latest book. I hope I have just gone past the middle of the narrative as I really am enjoying it and don't want to give it up. To get to settle into our (my husband Christopher and I) new lives we joined groups of activities that interested us and now feel truly settled here. However I still look in the mirror and see my English self. The two stories I have contributed have come from my "book of memories".

M. M. Jayne

M.M. Jayne is a Midwest writer and blogger. After serving in the U.S. Army Military Intelligence as a Russian Linguist and graduating from the University of Iowa with a degree in Soviet and East European Studies, she worked in management jobs until deciding to pursue a writing career. She is currently working on her first novel, Children of the Fragile Air, and blogs at www.thegreenstudy.com. She lives in the Twin Cities with her husband and daughter.

Mary Mitchell Lundeen

Mary Mitchell Lundeen lives with her husband, Jeff, in Elk River. Now semi-retired, Mary and Jeff enjoy visiting the State Parks of Minnesota in their camper. They also enjoy entertaining at their home and cruising on the pontoon. Mary and Jeff have two grown sons, one married, who live in the metro area. In retirement, Jeff is an artist who paints with oil and palette knife. Mary is a Licensed Psychologist gradually scaling back her work hours in order to allow other interests, such as writing with the Writer's Studio. Mary has written short stories and is working on a novel about a child with callous-unemotional traits.

Marj Helmer, Editor

(Marj Helmer on far right)

Helmer has been a student, high school teacher (German), mom, feminist, volunteer, office worker, computer trainer/sales/service, business owner, political candidate, grandma, and all around cheerleader. Currently she is a writer with rejections to prove it. She writes fiction based on important issues such as abortion (Mrs. A's Tea Party) and end-of-life decisions (Abide-A-While Resort.) She believes in the individual and learning as a life-long activity. She writes in Minnesota.

Caroline Munro

Caroline Munro has lived in Minnesota for twenty years but moved from England twenty five years ago, previously living in Atlanta, GA and Chicago, IL She studied Fashion Design in the UK specializing in knitwear design. Since moving to the US Caroline, has embraced many different Art forms, learning to quilt when her children were young, designing jewelry, learning to paint in watercolor and also designing mixed media embroidery.

Caroline took two classes at the Loft in Minneapolis, Memoir writing and Exploring different genres of writing. Since that time she has volunteered at the Maple Grove Art Center where she has curated textile shows, hosted fiber art studios and more recently helped start the Writers' Studio. It was during the weekly Writers Studio that she amalgamated her love of watercolor painting with a children's story she wrote "Magpies treasure" which she is in the process of illustrating.

Lise Spence-Parsons

Lise Spence-Parsons, a Brit ex-pat now residing in the Minneapolis suburbs, is a former accountant in the advertising world. Coming from an artistically based family, she has expanded her artistic journey into writing during the last eighteen months. Her love of social history and its effects on people has led to her writing her first novel based in London and northern France. She also enjoys writing short stories that enable the reader to think about issues and instances that they might not have explored previously. She intends to publish a collection of her short stories soon, followed by her novel.

Lise also spends time designing jewelry, watercolor painting and volunteers on a local community art center's board.

Sybil Swanson

Sybil Swanson has always loved reading. She also has loved to write little blurbs about what is happening in her life. One day, she met Marj Helmer. Marj asked Sybil if she was a writer. She answered no, she wasn't a writer of stories but was a reader. Marj said that was good enough. Sybil joined the Writers' Studio...the rest is history. She really looks forward to the weekly Writers' Studio meetings. So much to talk about; so much to learn about writing and what it takes to create a well-written piece. The Writers' Studio constitutes a wonderful, funny and totally serious bunch of writers.

Sybil doesn't limit her creative juices to writing. She also is an artist and paints almost every day. Whenever she can, she loves to teach acrylic fluid art. This she finds to be a very satisfying endeavor, especially when working with the elderly and handicapped as they learn to again "play in the paint" as they did when they were six.

You can connect with Sybil through e-mail at stswanson1@yahoo.com

Carolyn Wilhelm

Carolyn Wilhelm has a BS in Elementary Education, an MS in Special Studies of Gifted Children, and an MA in Curriculum and Instruction K-12. She was a National Board Certification Middle Childhood Generalist 2004-2014. She is also a licensed, certified teacher in Minnesota through 2021. Retired, she now volunteers at an elementary school. Carolyn is a wife, mom, and grandmother. One of her now-adult children was adopted from South Korea.

Recently, Carolyn and her daughter Betsy wrote A *Mom: What is an Adoptive Mother?* Her other self-published children's picture books include the following: *Alex Asks About Auntie's Airplane Day: An Adoption Day Story, Super Spoons to the Rescue; A Math Measuring Story,* and *The Frogs Buy A New House: An Economics Story for Children.* All her books are available on Amazon.

Gary L. Wilhelm

Gary L. Wilhelm is a retired engineer with a master's degree from South Dakota State University. He did research an development work in America, Asia, and Europe for consumer, commercial, and military products, during a career of several decades. In addition to being a civilian engineer embedded with the Marines during the Vietnam War in 1968 and 1969, he worked developing products ranging from EF Johnson Citizens band radio, and the Texas Instruments home computer, communications technology for use within buildings, and with medical devices implanted within the body, to the Howitzer Improvement Program (HIP) for army artillery on the battlefield. He was also a representative on a North Atlantic Treaty Organization (NATO) committee. He hosted the USA meeting of the committee at Honeywell.

He is the author of *Good Afternoon Vietnam: A Civilian in the Vietnam War*. His other book is for children and entitled, *Alex Asks Grandpa About the Olden Days: A 1940s Story*. Both are available on Amazon.

David Zander

David Zander is a Cultural Anthropologist who has worked with and written about many of the Asian Pacific refugees and immigrants in Minnesota. The Minnesota History Center has published and archived eight of his life histories of Hawaiians Samoans and Karen in Minnesota. He has published three small collections of Lao, Karen, and Cambodian (Khmer) folktales and personal stories told by refugees and monks in Minnesota published with the help of graphic design students from Dunwoody College. He has articles published in Asian American Press about Karen monks and was awarded a prize for his article the other face of Bhutan about Hindu refugees from Bhutan who fled to Nepal.

Left to right on the floor:
David Zander, Sybil Swanson, Lise Spence-Parsons, Caroline Munro,
Sarah Bromage, Marj Helmer
Up the stairs:
Gary Wilhelm, Carolyn Wilhelm, Laura Thompson.

Left to right:
Sarah Bromage, Sybil Swanson, Mary Mitchell Lundeen, David Zander
Photos by John S. Maciejny of Natural Images
johnnaturalimages@gmail.com

258

Made in the USA
Monee, IL
15 February 2020